PRINCESS

SOS

SARA PAGE

COVER DESIGNED AND CREATED BY ARIA
HTTP://RESPLENDENTMEDIA.COM/

CONTENTS

CHAPTER ONE

I'm going to die! I scream inside my head as the escape pod I'm currently riding in touches down, somewhere.

The impact rocks me to the core. Thankfully, I'm strapped into a very elaborate, very effective safety harness. Right now I can't move if I wanted to.

The dashboard in front of me flashes white and red with warning. Then a loud siren starts to blare. *As if I didn't know I was in deep shit!*

The pod starts to roll.

The shocks and protections of my harness and seat have kept me safe, thus far. My brain hasn't slipped around in my head. I didn't end up on the console as a splat. My body seems to still be in one piece instead of pieces. But now I'm trapped, helpless as the pod rolls and I roll along with it.

My stomach lurches as I go up and down, over and over. The escape pod must be rolling down a hill or something. *Stop, please stop. I'm going to be sick!*

My blood rushes to my head as I roll. My vision blurs, darkness is creeping in. Then it drops and I feel like I'm free falling.

There's another impact. The metal of the pod groans now with stress. The pod rolls once, twice. It pauses while I'm upside down. Figures just figures it would stop like this. Then one last rotation and I end up upright. The whole thing shudders then settles.

It's over. Bless the stars, it's over. I made it.

***

It takes several long minutes for my body to stop violently trembling. My lips are pressed together and my eyes are clenched shut as I hold back the sickness. If I throw up, it's going all over me. So I focus all of my energy in holding the sickness back.

Deep breath in, deep breath out.

I'm alive.

Deep breath in, deep breath out.

I'm not dead.

Slowly, I peek one eye open. The red and white warning lights are still flashing. My stomach gives a threatening lurch. I swallow the bile back.

I let my eyes adjust to seeing. After some time, I think my body can handle processing multiple senses. I feel safe enough to peek my other eye open.

The screen connected to the console is going crazy. All kinds of weird symbols and words are flashing, but to me, none of it makes any sense. All that I can think is that red must be bad. Something must be wrong with the pod, but even if I figure out what it is, I won't be able to fix it.

This is why princesses are not supposed to leave the planet.

My head starts to throb in tune with the rhythm of the blaring siren. If I want the noise to stop, I'm going to have free myself from my seat and do it.

I hold my breath for a moment. The rumbling in my stomach continues to ebb. Slowly, I release the breath and my fingers begin to slide across the straps of the harness, searching for the release.

Logically, I know the sound of the siren has remained steady, but as my fingers fail to find the harness release, and the throbbing in my head pounds harder and harder, it feels as if the siren grows louder and louder until I fear my ears themselves are about to explode.

Damn it all, how did I get myself into this thing?

The sickness is forgotten now as I frantically twist and turn, seeking out the magical button that will free me from the thing that just a few minutes ago kept me safe and whole. The button is nowhere to be found. My fingers search fruitlessly until I'm so frustrated, I end up screaming out.

"Just let me out! Please!"

Nothing happens. It would be too much to ask for voice activated control in such an outdated vessel. But I still hoped. My head drops forward in defeat. I cover my ears with my hands, but it's in vain. The siren is so loud I can feel it rattling my bones. I start to cry. I survived the crash only to die pathetically.

I'm so pathetic. I don't know how to operate an escape pod. I'm worthless. If they ever find me, I'll go down in history as the first princess to die by safety harness.

I let my tears flow freely but as my nose starts to drip, I instinctually wipe at it. Princesses don't drip snot all over themselves. What would the people think?

I wipe the snot hand on the skirt of my gown and then I use the back of my other hand to wipe at my eyes. I peek my eyes open for a moment, to try and clear them, and that's when I see it sitting right between my eyes: the harness release.

I press the release and then tear myself free of the safety belts. Stumbling forward, I almost fall, my knees unsteady, but I manage to get myself the four feet to the console.

I stare, stupidly, for too long at all the different buttons that make up the console. There's so much variety, so many sizes, and colors and none of them are labeled. I have no clue how to stop the siren, but there's one button that stands out. One giant red button that keeps blinking. That must be the button. It's red, all the strange letters scrolling across the screen are red. I bet it's blinking because that's the beat of the siren. It looks like an emergency button. It's the biggest.

I push the giant red button and the siren stops. *Yes!*

My ears are still ringing. It will probably be days before I can hear normally again. At first, I don't believe my ears as the ominous sound of air pressure releasing reaches them. I don't want to believe I heard that sound, I don't. But then I look up and sure enough, the pod is starting to open. There's a sky to be seen between the cracks.

No, no, no, no!

I thought dying trapped in the harness was bad, now it looks like I'm going to die from asphyxiation.

I don't know where I am. I don't know if there's any oxygen. The only way to tell would be to run a safety check before even daring to open the pod. Anything can be out there but now out there is coming in.

I inflate my lungs with air and hold it. I jam the button. I press it over and over again, trying to stop the process. Nothing happens. Desperately I consider the other buttons. There has to be a way to stop it, there has to be. There's another red button, though not quite as big. I push it.

The siren starts up again.

The walls of the pod shrink lower and lower. Bright rays of light beam inside, I squint my eyes against them.

I pound the smaller red button. Thankfully the siren stops. My lungs are burning. Spots are dancing in front of my eyes. Even if I can get the pod to close up again, I'll probably pass out.

This is it.

CHAPTER TWO

I can't keep it in. The air I was holding in my lungs bursts from me and I gasp in a shrill breath. It feels strangely good, the breath of fresh air. I expel and suck another mouthful in. The air tastes sweet… *Whoever thought air could be sweet?* How strange yet delightful.

The walls of the escape pod are fully down now. Now that I'm not dead, I realize very quickly that I'm fully exposed and very vulnerable. I look up to the sky, it's blue, just like home. And for a moment, I hope that somehow I am home.

This isn't home, I remind myself. But maybe this planet, wherever it is, is like home. And maybe if it is like home, maybe there are people that can help me.

I walk to the edge of the pod's floor and poke my head out where once there was a wall... There's green grass covering the ground. That too is just like home yet there's also patches of blue. We don't have blue grass where I come from.

I look off to the distance. There are hills upon hills, and vibrant vegetation. It looks like something out of the fairy tales I used to love to watch on the holovid when I was little. I peek a glance behind me. Yep, there are hills back there too, that's why I was rolling so much. You can clearly see the path the escape pod took, it left a huge swath of squished grass and colorful pressed plants. Even though the pod is resting at the base of a very tall hill, there's no hiding where it is.

I can hear the buzzing and hums of insects, so there's life besides the veggies. Thankfully I don't hear or see any animals.

To leave or not to leave?

I hesitate before stepping out.

Leaving is probably not a good idea. I'm not dressed or remotely prepared for exploring. I have no weapons to defend myself, nor any tools or instruments to give me direction. I'm wearing a pink party gown and satin slippers. I have no business stumbling about.

On the other hand, it's painfully obvious where my escape pod is, and I am escaping, I don't want to be found. If other ships are following me, they'll find me in an instant. I'm a sitting duck if I stay where I am right now.

I need supplies. There have to be supplies somewhere around here. Yet the escape pod is so ancient, it must be at least 50 years old. I wouldn't be surprised if whatever supplies there are supposed to be are rotted away by now.

The escape pod is a perfect circle. In the center of the circle is the safety seat. Four feet in front of the seat is the dashboard. You can't reach the dashboard or its console from the safety seat, which means once you're strapped in, you have no way to access the controls. In old escape pods, such as this one, it makes sense because those most likely to use the pods wouldn't understand the controls. The pods are programmed to automatically follow and steer a preprogrammed destination using advanced UPS. The technology is limited to automatic, though, unless you're a programmer and can overwrite the code. There's no way to manually pilot the vehicle, as far as I know.

To the right of the seat, I discover a box that serves as a type of portable potty and to the left of the seat I discover the bigger box that holds all of the emergency survival supplies. Among the supplies I find about a dozen hard things the size of bricks wrapped in foil, they're labeled as ration bars. There's also a sealed jug of water, two cups, a small first aid kit, a portable light, and a thin blanket.

All useful items, I'm sure, if you only need to survive in space while the pod autopilots you home, but there's nothing to help me survive in an alien wilderness.

It's probably best if I stick with the pod for a while.

Beneath the blanket I discover some paper. Thinking it's a manual or something that may help me with the console, I pull the pack of paper out. Lovely, just lovely. Some perverted soul left a vintage nudie mag. I put that back where I found it then move on to the front of the pod and start prodding around the dashboard.

Now that the siren isn't driving me to distraction, I explore the different buttons on the console.

I'm bent over, squinting at some faint lettering scratched above a black button when the hairs on the back of my neck stand up. I suddenly feel like I'm being watched. I whip around, with my heart thundering in my chest, and at first, I think I'm just being paranoid.

My eyes scan the horizon, everything looks as it did before. I don't see anything at first, then something moves in the corner of my vision. I turn my head and then I see it. It's the shape of a person, off in the far distance, coming around a hill.

I can't tell what kind of person it is at first, they're so far away, but they're moving fast. And I just have this feeling, this irrational fear or maybe it's a perfectly functioning instinct, that they mean to do me harm.

There's only one thing to do. I push the giant red button and hope with all my heart that the walls will go back up.

The shape of the person grows bigger and bigger. There's something oddly familiar about them yet something also very wrong. I squint my eyes and use my hand to shield them from the sun. I think it's a man, a huge giant of a man. He might be naked, he's definitely humanoid, but he's not the right color.

For several long seconds, nothing happens. I start jamming the button as if that could make it work.

Please go up walls.

If I had the guts to do it, I'd start pounding the other buttons as well but after the siren incident, I'm afraid I'll somehow make my situation worse.

Please, giant naked man running for me, please be a mirage.

I can't tear my eyes away from him, and it is definitely a him. I can see what makes it a male and not a female flopping as he runs. Holy shit, it's like a third leg.

I hear the screen behind me make several beeps. The sound of air pressure hissing in release this time is like music to my ears. The walls start to go up, but I'm not sure they're going up fast enough.

Giant man is coming closer and closer. He's purple and he's built like one of the elite soldiers in my father's personal squad. He could crush me like a puny lesser being and by the ferocious look on his face and his narrowed, glowing eyes, it looks like that's exactly what he means to do.

The walls reach my shoulders and then they go up and up until I can no longer see my approaching threat. He's so close, if he can jump, he can still get in. I'm so overcome with crippling fear, I feel paralyzed. I can't move my head, I can't look up and watch. I can only wait and hope he doesn't beat the walls.

Something slams into the side of the pod. I jump involuntarily and let out a startled scream. The pod rocks precariously. I look up. The walls are closed, he didn't make it in. *It must have been him crashing into the pod*, I think at first. But then something slams into the side again. *He's doing it on purpose. What the hell? Does he think he can go through flexible steel?*

He crashes into the side again. I almost expect to see a cartoonish imprint of his body. The pod rocks and almost rolls.

Oh, no. Not again.

I leap for the safety seat. I spent so much time trying to get out of the blasted thing, now all I want to do is get back in. My fingers shake, I'm operating on an overdose of adrenaline. My fumbling fingers manage to get half of my straps secured but then he slams and this time the pod rocks then starts to roll.

"No!" I scream out in terror as I'm forced upside down with only my left side secured in the harness.

I hold on for dear life, feeling gravity do everything in its power to pull me out of the seat as I'm forced upside down. My arms are crossed, my fingers dig into my own skin and it takes every bit of strength I have left to keep myself from falling.

As the pod rotates into its natural upright position, I feel myself drop against my seat. Franticly, I work on securing my right side. Just as I get the last strap secured, there's another crash and then I roll. This time the pod starts rolling and doesn't stop.

***

Growing up as a princess and the sole heir of the Terrea Kingdom and all that it encompasses, I was never permitted to ride amusement rides. They were deemed too risky and unnecessarily dangerous by my personal protection force. I've been to many amusement parks during my youth and often watched others of my age enjoy their experience. I never could quite understand how they found being thrown about or flipped upside down to be so fun. I especially couldn't understand how they could want to do it again and again.

Right now, being rolled over and over again is not my idea of fun. All I want is for it to stop because seriously, I'm about to throw up. But my luck must have run out. I keep rolling and rolling. Darkness creeps into the corners of my vision. I want to pass out. Oh, how I want to pass out. I want to wake up and have this all be over with but for some crazy reason my consciousness hangs on. By the time the pod finally stops, I can't even tell it has stopped at first. My brain keeps rotating, and my stomach is churning, stuck in the cycle, but my butt is no longer dropping.

I finally catch on.

This time it's a quick press of the release button and I'm out. I lurch to the side, throw open the portable potty box, and proceed to throw up my guts.

Everything comes out of me. I hack, gag, and heave until it feels like I'm expelling bits of my insides into the box. When I'm done, I slam the lid shut. I hope the biodegradable process in the box still functions. I'll know for sure the next time I open it up.

I stumble my way back to the dashboard. Déjà vu. Then I bend back over and double check the scratching I was reading above the black button before the charging purple alien man so rudely interrupted me.

The scratching above the button spells **HELP**. It could very well be a cry for help, but it's more likely that it's the button that accesses the pod's internal help system.

I hate buttons. Oh, my stars how I hate buttons now. I want to push it. I want to access the help system. I need to access the system. Accessing the system is the only way I'm going to be able to access the door so I can leave the pod without bringing all the walls down. It would also be nice to access any detection systems the pod may have. Maybe it can give me a UPS location, or a general idea of where I am. Or maybe there's a surveillance system that will allow me to see outside.

But I'm so scared. I'm so scared of what's going to happen. But what's the alternative? I can sit in here, in the dark, unable to see or know what's going on outside. The alien is most likely still outside. He could have tools, he could have a way to get in. He could have friends. I need to see. I need to access any systems the pod may have that I could use to scare him off or worse yet, defend myself.

I touch the button with my finger. Something so small, so normally insignificant, is now very much the difference between my life and death. I close my eyes and push the button.

The system beeps. I open my eyes and words I can actually understand flash across the screen. I navigate through the help system, pushing the buttons it indicates to cycle through the various options. I find the control for the door, the inside climate control, the current information on the outside conditions, and finally the pods exterior monitoring and surveillance system. I cycle the surveillance system to **ON** and then half of the console's screen fills up with two pictures of outside.

The two pictures show either side of the pod. On the left side there appear to be trees. It's darker outside and becoming harder to see. The only lighting on the outside of the pod is its flashing built in lights and reflectors. They're used mainly so other ships can see and avoid collision with the vessel. The lights are not nearly strong enough to illuminate more than a few inches.

On the right side of the pod is the mean purple alien. He looks even more frightening bathed in the pod's glowing red lights. *Like a space demon.* He's staring at the pod as if he's perplexed. His arms are crossed over his broad chest and his brow is furrowed. No doubt he's trying to figure out a way in.

I start cycling through the pod's system options. I go through audio, discover the siren controls and quickly toggle them off. After some more digging around in the menus, I finally unearth an intercom system.

I press the blue button that resembles the one mirrored on the screen and say, "Hey."

The alien jumps, startled. His reaction is very satisfying.

I push the button again and say, "Go away."

This time he cocks his head to the side.

I push the button and say, "Go away," again, so he understands.

The alien starts to smack the side of his head. I'm not sure what to make of that.

Being able to talk to him and him not being able to get to me gives me a false sense of security. I take the opportunity to really check him out.

He's big, oh yes, he's big. I can't help but stare there, at the thing that dangles between his legs. I've never really seen one before, a man's penis. I've seen animals and I've seen drawings but never seen a real life one in high definition. It's a lot uglier than I imagined, yet, there's something about it I find strangely appealing.

My eyes slide up, over the v of his hips and then up the rippled expanse of his chest. Every inch of him appears to be solid muscle. From the bulges in his arms to the thick meat of his thighs, he's hard and sculpted all over.

He's a machine, a killing machine, I think as I take in the hard lines of his face and his menacing glowing red eyes. A body like that isn't natural, it's obtained and maintained, and in this environment, it must be because he's a natural born predator. *I must be the prey.*

I shiver and cross my arms over my chest. There's something so familiar about him, he's entirely too human looking. If he wasn't purple, and it's not even a vibrant purple, it's more that he's purple in all the places that I'm pink. And if he didn't have the freaky eyes, I could totally mistake him for one of my own kind.

The alien steps up to the pod and places his hands against it. He begins to run his hands over the pod as if he's searching for something. I bet he's searching for a way inside.

I uncross my arms and push the blue button again, "Hey, you. Do you understand Galactic?"

He stops, cocks his head again but doesn't respond.

I sigh. I want to assume his lack of response means he just doesn't understand what I'm saying but there's also the possibility that he does understand, he's just not going to let me know it.

"I am Princess Ameia, daughter of Trivent the current sovereign of Terrea. My people are on their way to aid me. If you are still here when they arrive, they will use lethal force against you."

Okay, so the last bit was a bit of a bluff but I really need him to think it's not a good idea to keep messing around with me. If he even does understand me.

He takes a step back, away from the pod, yet his glowing eyes continue to bore into it. I hold my breath, waiting, hoping he'll decide I'm too much trouble.

Outside, it continues to grow darker and darker. Inside the pod, the temperature feels like it's dropping. I can't stop shivering. Outside, it must be just as cold yet the naked alien man doesn't appear to be the least bit affected by it. The seconds tick by until it feels like minutes have passed. My heart is thumping like a drum in my ears. *Go, just go*, I mentally urge him.

He takes a step towards the pod, I almost cry out with disappointment. Then he seems to think better about it and turns away. I blink, and he disappears into the darkness.

I thought I would be relieved to see him go. I let go of the breath I was holding. But now that he's gone, I only feel more nervous. Maybe it would have been better if I had just kept him where I could see him.

CHAPTER THREE

The thin blanket left in the storage box is surprisingly warm. I wrap myself in it and spend the rest of the night in the seat, dozing off then jerking awake. I keep dreading, even in my dreams that the alien will return. At one point, I even strap myself back up in the safety harness. If he does return and starts rolling the pod again, at least I'll be somewhat prepared. At least I won't die right away.

I'm not sure how much time has passed when I do finally decide to stay awake. It's light outside. There's a clock in the computer system, but it's not set, it blinks zero, and I'm afraid of messing with anything I don't understand.

My stomach growls so I unstrap myself and grab one of the foil wrapped bricks out of the storage box. I think this is probably the longest time I've gone without eating. I try to think of the last meal I had. Oh, yes, I had some finger foods at my birthday party but then Vrillum pulled me away.

The bar is so hard I can't even take a bite out of it. I scrape at it with my teeth. It's a dark mossy green color, probably packed with iron and protein, but it tastes so bitter I cough and almost choke. I wrap the brick back up and return it to the box then pull out a cup and the jug of water.

The water at least is sealed and seems to be
okay. I gulp down two cups and feel a little better.
The hunger eases. I think I might be able to survive
without food for a couple of days. If I can find a
way in the pod's system to contact my father, I may
only have to hold out for a few hours.

I spend the day searching through the various
help functions, searching for a way to communicate
or send a signal. After a few hours, I start to develop
a creak in my neck from the way I'm standing and
my back hurts from bending over. Then my eyes
start to blur with strain. I plop myself down on the
safety seat and take a break.

I don't know what to do. I don't even know
what I'm doing. My stomach rumbles. I'm not used
to going hungry. I drink a couple more cups of
water, but I still need something to eat.

*Maybe if I mix some of the bar with the water I'll be
able to get it down without gagging.*

I scrape the bar against the edge of the box,
filling the cup with mossy green shavings. When
the bottom of the cup is covered, I then fill it up
with water but the shavings stay stuck to the
bottom. Maybe if it has some time to sit, it will
soften. I rest the cup on the floor and wait.

After a while, I pick the cup up and swirl it around. The shavings have turned into a thick green sludge. It doesn't look the least bit appetizing, but it's all I have. My stomach rumbles again, I have to eat something. I pinch my nose and lift the cup to my lips. I tip my head back and drink. The water is easy but once it's gone, the sludge is slow and sticky. I swallow it, just barely, and then chase it down with a bunch more water. Hands down it's the worst thing I've ever eaten, or drank for that matter. The hunger goes away, but I'm stuck with a very bad taste in my mouth.

The rest of the day is uneventful. Once it starts to grow dark outside once more, I strap myself back into the seat and wait. I fall asleep and stay asleep until morning.

***

I wake up. I must have slept very deeply and very peaceful because I was drooling. I wipe my mouth off with my hand and check the screen for any signs of life outside. It's been a day now since I've seen the alien. If he came around last night, I think it would have disturbed me.

I take care of my business in the portable potty box. Thankfully the box does break down biowaste, so it's not filling up the pod with a stink. The stink that's starting to permeate through the pod is definitely coming from me. I need a wash, but I know it wouldn't be a good use of the water I have left. Between using the water when I'm both hungry and thirsty, I've already gone through half the jug. If I'm not careful, I won't have any water left by tomorrow morning.

I spend the rest of the day messing around with the help system, going through all the selections again and again, just trying to keep myself occupied throughout all this waiting.

I'm waiting for everything. Waiting for someone to help me. Waiting for the alien to reappear. Waiting for my water to run out. Waiting to go hungry. All this waiting is driving me so crazy. I'm just waiting for something to happen. Waiting for anything.

If I'm not waiting, I'm worrying.

Why has no one come yet? Surely my father must be looking for me... It doesn't make any sense. Vrillum didn't take us out that far out. Whatever planet I crashed on must be only hours away from home. The UPS of the escape pod should easily be within range.

Something is wrong, very wrong. *Perhaps the UPS in the escape pod isn't working...* It's a sad fact that I find that thought even remotely reassuring, especially when compared to the other possibilities. I rather think that I'm stuck on this planet because of the ancient, decrepit escape pod's malfunctioning capabilities then think I'm still here because no one is trying to come for me.

As the hours creep on, I start to feel like the walls of the pod are starting to close in on me. For an escape pod, it's actually quite roomy. That's why it's designed the way it is, a perfect circle with retractable walls. On a ship, they're stored with the walls down. They stack up like discs, then one by one the walls go up and the pods go shooting out into space when activated. But even for a roomy escape pod, it's too small. I need fresh air. I need to move.

If the alien doesn't come back tonight, I'm going to venture out tomorrow morning. I hope I don't have to. I hope help arrives and I'm home by tomorrow morning.

Hopefully, this just that story I'll tell my Grandkids when I'm older. *Gather round, kiddies, let Grandma tell you about the time she crash landed on a remote planet and was chased by a purple alien with a huge penis. She survived with only sludge bars and a porta potty...*

After another sludge dinner, I strap myself in the safety harness and spend the night sleeping fitfully. I dream of glowing eyes and crashing ships. Still, morning comes too quickly.

CHAPTER FOUR

There's no sign of help when I wake up. On the bright side, there's no sign of the alien either. It's not lost on me that this entire time I've been sitting in the pod, watching and waiting, there hasn't been a sign of much of anything going on. I'm going to take it as a good sign, though, there must not be much outside, or at least in this area that can hurt me.

I'm not dressed for exploring and there's not much I can do to remedy the situation, but I do decide to arm myself with one of the foil covered bricks. *Worse comes to worse, I can threaten to force feed it to them.*

By now, I have almost all the buttons of the console and their related functions burned into my memory. It's a simple push of a green button and part of one of the retractable walls hisses and drops down, disappearing into the floor. The gap left in its place serves as my door to outside.

Fresh air fills the pod, airing out my stink. Breathing it in, I'm reminded that it tastes strangely sweet. The first time I tasted it, it was new and refreshing. This time the sweetness is only making me more hungry.

Wanting to leave is one thing, actually doing it is another. I cast one last glance at the console screen. The area surrounding the escape pod is still empty. I walk up to the gap in the walls and peek my head outside. I wait and listen. I don't hear anything but bugs hissing and chirping.

I stick one foot out and wait. Nothing happens so I step outside. I'm surrounded by trees. The trees look like normal trees to me. Most of them seem to be really old with thick brown trunks that reach high into the blue sky. Like the grass, their branches are covered in blue and green leaves. I wait another moment, in case something starts to come after me. When nothing does, I walk around the pod and look to the other side, expecting to see the path the pod squashed.

How did he roll me through the trees without crashing? There's no sign of the path the pod took. No knocked over trees or even trampled plants. I circle the pod to be sure. I remember the rolling, remember it quite vividly. I was rolling fast and didn't feel as if any of it was controlled. Yet the alien must have obviously maneuvered the pod. I can't even tell which direction the pod came from.

Why here? Why roll the pod here? Because of all the trees?

If I wanted to hide the pod, this would be the perfect place. Even from the sky it would be difficult to spot with all the leaves of the trees forming a thick canopy. This doesn't bode well for me. Maybe this is why my help hasn't been able to find me.

I walk back to the gap in the wall. I need to be closer to safety, I'm starting to get very creeped out. My eyes search through the trees, looking for anything that could be out of place. Maybe I'm just being paranoid but I get the feeling I'm not alone.

Is he out there? Watching me? Planning something?

I shiver at the thought. I hurry back inside the pod and push the little button, bringing the wall back up. I look to the screen, half expecting to see the alien coming out of the trees, making a run to get inside.

When the alien rolled the pod here, he must have been planning something at the time. If he is watching, how many days do I have until he thinks no one is coming to help me?

How many days until I?

***

I think the green sludge dinners are giving me bad dreams. Last night, after securing myself in the safety seat, I dreamt of the Reavers.

I dreamt that after another day of searching through the pod's help system, I finally stumbled upon its deep space communication system. I sent out an SOS, hoping it would reach someone from my homeworld, preferably my father.

Hours later, a ship arrived but it wasn't a ship I was familiar with. In horror, I watched as a group of Reavers, clad in their notorious obsidian body armor, encircled my pod and demanded in short, barking Galactic orders that I surrender and present myself.

The Reavers are the boogeymen of space. They're the specific reason on my homeworld, princesses are not permitted to leave the planet. Not only are they unmatched on the battlefield, decimating any enemy that stands in their way, but they're infamous for stealing females of other species. Rumored to have no females of their own.

My great, great Aunt was carried off by a Reaver before the princess decree was put into place. She was the legitimate heir to the throne, traveling to her betroths homeworld for an official introduction. Her ship was intercepted somewhere along the way, and neither she nor the crew were ever heard of again.

In my dream, I was frozen in fear. I wanted to move, but I couldn't. I wanted to present myself and beg on my knees, as a princess, to please spare me. To please ransom me to my father, he would pay whatever was demanded.

The Reavers cut into the flexible steel walls of the pod with laser knives. Then one Reaver entered. I couldn't move. I couldn't run. I couldn't hide. I couldn't even scream. All I could do was quake with terror, completely impotent as it grabbed me.

The Reaver pulled me close, slamming me roughly into the hard obsidian plate covering its chest. Then it looked down at me and grinned. That's when I realized it was missing the gruesome horned helmet they were so fond of. That's when I could see the Reaver was purple with red glowing eyes.

"Mine," the Reaver said then kissed me.

I awoke with a scream.

CHAPTER FIVE

For the first time since I've crashed, I'm in utter despair. I awoke, disturbed and afraid after my nightmare. But then, after the fear wore off and I realized I was still very much alone, I started to cry.

I can't stop crying.

No one is coming for me. It's been what, four days? Five? I'm Princess Ameia, beloved daughter of Trivent, sole heir to the Kingdom of Terrea. Someone should be looking for me... but if they were, I would have been found by now.

I'll never see my father again, or my friends. I'll never go home again. I'm stuck here, all alone. I'll die strapped to the safety seat, sitting next to a portable potty. That's how they'll find me. *If someone ever does.*

I don't know what to do. I don't know how to survive. I'm still dressed in this pretty pink gown I wore to my birthday party and my best satin slippers. I have plenty of rock hard, probably expired ration bars, but I'm almost out of water. The only way to get more water is by going out and looking for it.

I cry because I'm alone and afraid, and everything feels helpless. My nose starts to drip and I just let it. I cry because I'll spend the rest of my life eating sludge dinners. I cry because I'm starting to get thirsty and I only have a little water left, but I don't want to drink it.

Once the water is gone, it's the end. I'm dead. But then, if I'm dead anyway, why not die while looking for more?

Gradually, my will and reason starts to come back to me. I start to realize I'm feeling sorry for myself and that things could be so much worse. I grab on to that fact for dear life. *Things could be worse. I still have a chance if I take it.*

Whenever I used to cry at home, there was someone always quick to chastise me for it. More often than not it would have been my nanny chastising me when I was younger, and occasionally, when he could find the time, it would be my father. But as I grew older, I learned to do it myself. I am a princess, they would often remind me, unmoved by my tears. I was born into privilege and destined for greatness, what were my troubles when compared to others? Princesses do not cry, princesses are above crying. If there is a problem, we fix it. If we cannot fix it, we move on.

I feel drained, but a little bit relieved after getting all the tears out. It was like I was holding too much inside me and just needed to relieve the pressure by letting go of some of it. Now that the pressure is out of the way, I can think a little better.

Perhaps, there is still hope.

I wipe at my nose, drink a little bit of my water, and then check the surveillance cameras. It's light outside. Nothing has moved for days. If I'm careful, I can go out and search. There's so much vegetation about, there should be at least one source of water nearby. Hopefully.

I eye my jug of water, there's only about an inch left on the bottom. I check the screen again, the conditions outside haven't changed.

What am I waiting for? Now or never, I can do this. I stand up, gripping the jug.

I need to do this before I lose my nerve.

If nothing moves outside, if there's no sign of the alien man, I'll search the surrounding area for water. I'll stay close to the pod, so I don't get lost. I'll just walk out a span or so and see what I can find.

I walk up to the dashboard and push the green button on the console. There's a hiss and then part of the wall lowers down, disappearing into the floor. Just like before, sweet, fresh air flows into the pod and I greedily breathe it in. I didn't quite realize how stuffy and stagnant it was in here until now. Maybe, while I'm gone everything will air out. *Who are you kidding? Your stinky princess funk is forever imprinted in this pod. They'll have to burn it.*

Still gripping my jug in my hand, I step out and down. Rays of sunlight beam through the thick canopy of leaves overhead, I welcome the warmth. It feels good to be outside, in the sun, instead of surrounded by metal. My eyes scan my surroundings, but nothing moves. I wait another couple of minutes just to be sure.

Part of me wants there to be a disturbance, I think. It makes me hesitate. It's the part of me that's still afraid, the part that wants to run back into the pod to hide and die. But I don't want to die, I remind myself, I want to live. So I put one foot in front of the other and I don't look back. I keep my eyes forward.

I walk half a span away and nothing happens. The biggest obstacle so far is not tripping over fallen branches and tree roots. I keep walking, carefully, while keeping an ear out. There's strange buzzes, hums, and clicks that I've always assumed were just insects. But now that I'm out here, and taking in how different this place truly is compared to my home planet, I realize those sounds could just as likely come from animals.

I turn back and discover I walked further than I intended to. As I see just how far away I am from my unprotected pod, panic's icy fingers start to grip my heart. I start to rush more than I should, but I manage to make it back to the pod with my only hiccup being a stubbed toe.

Nothing happens when I get there, still there is no one around. I start to feel silly for all my worrying. Perhaps it is true in this situation that the only thing to fear is fear itself.

I set out to search for water from the other side of the pod. If I keep the pod at my back, all I have to do is turn around and look for it to keep from getting lost. I get to about half a span away when I hear it, fresh flowing water must be nearby. I can hear it bubbling and splashing against what I assume are rocks. If I breathe in deeply enough, I can even smell it.

I start to get excited and I start to rush. I follow my ears forward and before I know it, I've gone another half a span and then more. I find the pool of water tucked behind a tight grouping of trees. As I come upon it, small, fuzzy creatures scurry off, disturbed by my presence, into the brush.

My first glimpse of animals reminds me that I need to slow down and pay attention. There are other things about, and they're not so fuzzy, and not so quick to scurry at the sight of me.

Cautiously, I approach the pool of water and then bend down. The water is clear and appears to be clean but the reflection mirrored back to me gives me a scare.

No wonder I frightened off the local wildlife, sheesh.

I stare into the water and I can hardly recognize myself. The woman staring back at me is not the poised young woman I know. It's like looking at a complete stranger. A stranger who is disheveled and dirty with her oily blonde curls clinging to her face and tangling around her ears. At one time, her blue eyes probably glittered like dark sapphires but now her eyes are puffy and tired and stained with dark circles. I splash my fingers in the water to make her disappear. Then I lift my fingers to my lips to taste the water.

Something hits me in the back of the head and I cry out, "Ow!"

I look down and there's a small fruit of some sort. I pick it up, it's red and soft but when it hit my head, it sure hurt like it was hard. I look up to see if perhaps it fell down. But none of the trees appear to be fruit bearing trees and I don't see any other fruits hanging from the branches or growing from the ground.

Maybe it's my lucky day and not only did I find water but I scored some yummy food as well?

I hang on to the fruit and bend back down. I start to dip my jug into the water when something hits me in the back of the head again.

"Hey!" I cry out this time and spin around.

I don't know what I was expecting to find, maybe an ornery monkey or something? Certainly not the big, scary alien guy I see staring angrily at me.

I don't even think about it, I just run. I push my way through the brush, stumble over the bumps and stub my toes on the rocks. My gown catches, snagging on the branches, but I don't stop, I let it tear.

I can hear him behind me, growling and yelling something in his alien tongue. If I slow down for a second, I know he'll catch me. I don't understand a word he's saying, but if I had to guess, I guess it would be something about killing me or eating me, or perhaps something even worse.

My lungs burn, my knees ache, but I don't stop until I make it back to the pod. I jump through the opening and pray to the stars I can close the door before he catches up. I hit the green button and spin back around.

He's almost there, he's reaching for me. The wall is going up. His hand goes over the top, then it blindly searches for something to latch on. I jump back and watch. Up, up the wall goes. He's tall but if he doesn't pull his hand back in the next couple of seconds, it's soon going to join me in the pod, alone.

The alien yanks his hand back and roars loudly in his alien tongue. The wall reaches the top. The pod is fully closed. I'm safe. I sag in relief against the console.

I catch my breath for a minute and then watch him on the screen. He's stares angrily at the wall, huffing. I half expect him to start crashing into the pod again, and consider strapping myself into the safety seat. Before I move, he turns his head and I swear his glowing eyes are staring at me. It's as if he can see me, the way he is looking at me. Our eyes are locked, we're face to face. His lips even begin to curve into a knowing smile. *What the hell?* I'm so frightened about what's going on, I hit the button for the surveillance system and turn it off.

He can't see me. He can't see through the metal, I tell myself. But cold shivers travel down my spine. I'm seriously creeped out.

I still strap myself into the safety seat, just in case. I know he's still out there. I can feel it. I know, too, that I won't be able to relax until he's gone. A minute later, I get thirsty and reach for my jug. It's not there in its usual spot. Oh no, oh no. I must have dropped it back at the pool of water.

Now I'm really fucked.

CHAPTER SIX

I'm going to die. Maybe I'm going insane but I don't feel upset over it. I feel more like I've been waiting for this, that it's been inevitable. Don't get me wrong, I don't want to die. I want to live. If a ship from Terrea suddenly touched down, I'd gladly board it. I want nothing more than to be rescued and returned to my home. But the grim reality is that I have only hours left, if even that.

I'm out of water. I have plenty of ration bars to eat, but I don't dare even try to gnaw on them because I know their bitter nastiness will only make me thirstier.

Daylight has come. I've rested as best as I could. The question now is how do I want to die?

Do I stay here, locked in my little pod, and wither away alone? Or do I go out fighting?

I've never been much of a fighter. I've always had others ready to fight and die for me. I don't think anyone has ever encouraged or wanted me to fight for myself. I've turned the surveillance system back on. All has been quiet. But I know he's out there. It's the type of knowing I can feel in my bones. He's out there, hiding, watching, and waiting for me to come out.

I arm myself with a ration bar. It's as hard as a brick and it's all I've got. I'll fight him if I have to, but I have no delusions who will win if it comes to that. My only hope right now is that I can somehow make it to my water jug and back to the pod without him noticing.

I hit the green button and the wall drops down, disappearing into the floor. I take a step out and freeze. I don't know what I was expecting. I think I was expecting this time to be much like the last, that I'd walk out, there would be no sign of him, and I would gain the courage to explore.

I certainly wasn't expecting to see him out there in the distance, crouched and watching me.

He doesn't blend. His purple contrasts too much against the brown, blue, and green of the surrounding forest. He rises slowly, vaguely I realize he's wearing pants. He begins to walk towards me.

I lose all my nerve.

I jump back and pound the green button. The wall begins to slide up. I turn my eyes to watch him on the screen. I know he sees the wall, but he doesn't rush. If anything, it looks like he's taking his time. He's sauntering, confidently. It's kinda starting to piss me off.

"Damn you," I curse at the screen. My throat is dry and my voice sounds scratchy.

If it wasn't for him, I wouldn't be in this situation. I'd have water. I'd have so much time left, days, maybe even weeks, to wait for a rescue.

This is all his fault. I want to scream in
frustration, but I know it would only make my
throat hurt worse. *Damn you giant, purple alien man.*

I throw the ration brick at the wall. It connects
with a thud then bounces back. The cursed thing
hits me in the head. Now, not only am I cursing in a
very unprincess like manner but I'm also crying.

I hate crying.

I'm a coward. His appearance has reminded me
of that. My situation hasn't changed. I'm still
without water but instead of injecting myself with
false bravado, and convincing myself that I'm
capable of doing things I am so not capable of
doing, I'll not only die here, pathetically, I'll go out
knowing I didn't even try to save myself.

I hate him. I hate him so much that I'm shaking
with it. I hate what he's done to me, hate how he's
tortured me. I hate how he's made me see myself.

I want to push the green button and lob this
ration brick right at his head. I'm reaching for the
green button when I glimpse the screen and pause.

Something is different.

Not only is he wearing pants, black very tight
fitting pants but he's holding something in his hand.
How did I not notice that?

Again, he looks at the camera as if he's looking
directly at me. He bends down, his glowing eyes
never leaving mine and rests my water jug just
outside the door. He straightens, turns away, and
walks off, disappearing into the forest.

What just happened? Did I just imagine that?

I wait, and I wait. I'm so sick of waiting. I'm half convinced he brought the water jug as a means for me to open the wall, but I had the wall down. I can't make sense of it.

The jug is full of water. I can see it. I can't stop staring at it on my screen. I lick my dry lips.

It must be poisoned or drugged. Why else give me a means to survive longer inside here?

It's a trick. Maybe I'll push the button, the wall will go down, and the jug won't even be there.

I do just that. I push the button and the wall goes down. I'm surprised that the jug is there. I'm even more surprised when my fingers wrap around it and lift it. It's very much real. I pull the jug in while my eyes scan the forest. There's nothing, no movement. I pull the jug in, push the button, and the wall goes back up without incident.

To drink or not to drink?

I open the jug and sniff at it. It smells like water. If it's drugged, perhaps I'll taste it. I dip my finger in the water, it's blessedly cold. I suck the drops of water from my finger. It's delicious. I dip my finger in, again and again. Before I know it I'm lifting the jug to my mouth and drinking directly from it.

Swallow after swallow, I drink until I'm sated. I didn't mean to do it but I was so thirsty and it was such a small pleasure to drink. I have so few pleasures now.

I put the jug back in its rightful place and take my seat, but I don't put on the safety harness. I wait until I'm falling asleep next to my portable potty. You know, just in case I need it.

CHAPTER SEVEN

He's kissing me. It's not the Reaver. This time it's the big, purple alien. He's naked again and he's so hard. He pushes himself against me and I find I actually quite like it.

I like the way he feels. I like the way our hips lock. We fit together as if we were made to fit.

There's strength in his hardness. A strength that will protect me. My hands roam over him, exploring and committing him to memory. I trace the ridges of his muscles and follow the grooves of his battle scars. From the look of him, I imagined his flesh would be thick and stiff, more like leather. I'm pleasantly surprised to discover his purple skin is silky soft. My fingers slip and slide all over him.

His mouth slants over my mouth. He's so hungry and so warm as he kisses me. He's kissing me as if he can't get enough.

He's sweet, the sweetest thing I've eaten in days. I make a small sound in my throat. I want to bite him. I want to sink my teeth into him.

I sink my nails into his back instead.

He seems to like this. His kiss becomes more desperate. I feel his hands gripping my hips, kneading them. I squirm, my stomach tightens. His hands slide around my hips and he grabs up handfuls of my ass. I moan into his kiss. My core clenches

He grinds his hips against my sex and the shock of it wakes me up.

My heart is racing inside my chest. My eyes dart around my pod, looking for him.

It's just me, all by my lonesome.

Was it a dream? It felt so real.

I'm covered in a film of sweat, all hot and bothered. There's a steady, familiar ache between my thighs. I squeeze my legs together, very embarrassed.

Did I seriously just have a wet dream about the space demon?

***

I know I've gone off the deep end now. I've been trapped, alone in this pod, going insane for too long. Especially if I'm having wet dreams about the scary alien who looks like he rather break me then kiss me.

I feel sick, and a bit perverted my mind even went there. I mean, seriously, how could I have a wet dream, a vivid sexual fantasy about *him*? He wants to kill me for fuck sakes. What is wrong with me?

I've heard of space madness, when people get stuck in space for days, weeks, or years at a time, all alone. They start to have delusions and hallucinations, losing touch with reality. Sometimes they recover when they reunite with civilization. Sometimes they never come back.

Maybe I'm suffering space madness. The thought frightens me just as much as dying does. Losing my mind, going crazy while I'm trapped in this pod....

I need air. I need sky above me and ground below me. But I can't have it because that damn alien is out there, being a creepy, psycho killer stalker.

Maybe just a few minutes will be enough. If I open the door, stand outside and tuck tail as soon as I see him, I should be okay. It's worked so far.

I grab my jug to take a drink first. I start to lift it to my lips then stop, eyeing it suspiciously. Maybe the water is drugged. Maybe he put some weird alien drug in it to make me dream of him. I smell the water. It smells like water. Maybe I should just stop with the maybes and focus on taking care of myself.

I drink from the jug and then check the surveillance camera.

Huh? That's weird.

I hit the green button and the wall sinks into the floor. Just outside the gap, on the ground, are two red fruits.

Are those the fruits that hit me in the head?

I poke my head out and scan my surroundings. I don't see anything. Cautiously, I step out of the pod. I walk up to the fruits and toe them with my slipper. They roll to the side and otherwise nothing happens.

I bend over and pick the fruit up. For a moment, I wondered if they were just a mirage. But no, the fruit is very real as my hands cover them. I straighten and weigh the fruits in my hands.

This doesn't make any sense. I don't know what to make of it. Why did he bring me food? Is it a peace offering? Is it to get me to let my guard down? Should I even take it?

I tip my head back and look to the sky. I watch the leaves flutter and sway in the breeze. It feels so good to be outside, I just have to soak it all in. I suck in a lungful of air. It smells so good to be outside. It's just as sweet as I remembered it.

I can't take the fruit, especially because I don't know what it means.

Through the leaves, I can see clouds rolling across the blue sky. Hungrily, my eyes watch them scroll past.

I don't know how long I stood there, watching the clouds, but it felt really good. It felt as good as drinking the water after I had gone thirsty for all that time. This was another need, being outside, in the open. I need to be sure I don't neglect it.

I knew he would be there when I finally dragged my eyes away from the sky. I knew it and dreaded it.

As soon as my eyes touch upon him, I can't help but fear him. He's so scary looking. Every fiber in my body is screaming at me, telling me to run, yelling that's he's going to kill me. He's seven feet tall, purple, and staring at me with glowing red eyes.

He just might be trying to fatten me up before he decides to eat me. Little pig, little pig, let me in...

The alien doesn't move for me, though. He keeps his distance and there's such intensity in the way he holds himself, such rigidness. His hands clench at his sides and I get the impression he's holding himself back. I get the feeling he wants to pounce on me and the longer I stand here, the more likely it's going to happen.

I open my hands and the fruit falls to the ground. Something akin to confusion passes over his stern features. His lips pull into a frown. I shiver, it only makes him look scarier.

I turn and tuck tail back to my pod. I hit the green button and turn to watch the wall go back up. I half expect him to come after me, but he doesn't. I can't see him on the surveillance camera and he doesn't approach close enough for me to see him.

Once the wall reaches the top, I let out the breath I didn't realize I was holding.

I had a wet dream about that? About that? If my rescue doesn't come soon, I might as well end myself.

CHAPTER EIGHT

That night, thankfully, I don't dream. I do, however, wake up with a stiff neck. Life in the pod is becoming more and more unbearable. It's incredibly difficult to get comfortable and I'm really starting to feel gross.

I have enough food and water for the time, but I need to find a way to wash myself and my clothes. If I don't, I'm going to get sick.

The alien can't be watching me all the time. The light bulb goes off over my head after I choke down a green sludge lunch. He has needs as well and I doubt he can see to them all while watching the pod.

So I start experimenting.

Today, at random times, I steel myself and begin to step outside the pod to wait for the alien to show up. I'm hoping a pattern will develop. Maybe, after a couple of days, I'll get a feel for his routine if he has one. Or if I'm really lucky, something awful will happen to him and I won't have to worry at all.

I step out after lunch. He doesn't show up for almost thirty minutes. I step out later in the afternoon and he shows up rather quickly. I step out just as it looks as if it's getting dark and he shows up within a minute.

That night, I toss and turn on the floor. I don't get much sleep. Early in the morning, I step out and he doesn't show up at all. An hour passes then another, there's no sign of him. I seriously start to get my hopes up. He's not coming. Either he gave up or something happened to him.

I'm just about to throw myself a little party when he makes an appearance. Dang it. I look up and note the sun is high in the sky. It must have just transitioned from morning to afternoon. I make a mental note of it.

***

I pop out later that afternoon and again the alien shows up rather quickly. I wonder if he's catching on to what I'm doing. That evening, he's there as soon as I open the door, standing just in front of the trees. He's closer and it's a little disturbing. But what's even more disturbing is that he's left me another offering. The two red fruits are back, placed a couple of feet away from the pod. Balanced on top of the fruit is a stick and skewed on the stick is some kind of cooked meat.

My stomach growls, loudly. My mouth starts to water. I want it, bad. I feel his intense glowing eyes on me. My eyes dart to him then back to the meat. Is it a trap? It feels like a trap.

My stomach doesn't care, it wants me to grab it and eat.

It was so much easier to refuse the fruit. The fruit is strange, it could be sour instead of sweet for all I know. It doesn't smell delicious. The fruit doesn't have crispy, crunchy, yummy looking skin. The fruit isn't dripping mouthwatering, stomach burning juices.

I take one step forward, testing him. He doesn't move. He just watches me as he always has, tense, holding himself back as if he's on the verge of charging me.

I take another step forward. I feel so uncomfortable moving away from my pod, moving closer to him. Another step and I'm almost there. I swear I can almost see a vein, a dark purple vein, throbbing in his neck.

He's going to make a move, I just know it. He's the hunter, I'm the prey. The food is the trap. I'm an idiot.

I take a step back. He looks furious.

I take another step back. He straightens, somehow drawing himself up taller, and barks out something in his alien tongue. I have no idea what he's saying but the noises he's making sound angry to me.

I take another step back and he starts walking for me.

Yep, I'm done now. I scramble back into the pod
and jam the green button. I watch on the screen as
he stomps up to the fruit and skewer. He picks up
the stick with the meat on it and looks to the
camera, doing that unnerving thing where it's like
he's staring right at me.

He jabs the meat in the air and says something. I
just can't wrap my head around the language. It's
like a mixture of clicks, grunts, and coughs. It makes
absolutely no sense.

He stands, holding the stick in the air as if he's
waiting for me to respond. The meat starts to slide
down the stick. I just want to cry watching it. I
could have had that meat, that crispy, tender, juicy
meat. *But then he would have me.* My stomach
clenches, it's so mad. I'll just have to smother it with
a bunch of water and green sludge.

The alien grunts out something loudly. I'm
thinking it was a curse word. He looks at the meat,
then back to me, then to the meat again. Abruptly,
he turns away and stomps over to the fruit. He
bends over to pick up the fruit, and the sick, pervert
that I am, I find myself checking out his ass.

Where did he get pants? Why is he wearing pants?
It's unsettling. It makes him look that much less
savage. He's a savage. Don't forget it, Ameia. Even
if he's a savage with a yummy stick of meat and
nice ass.

With one hand, he grabs the two fruits. He could crush my skull with that one hand. He turns around and stomps back to the spot he was just standing in. Now he lifts both the stick and the fruit in the air and says something in his alien gibberish. Then, purposely, he bends down. He puts the fruit down then balances the meat on top of it. Once he has it set up, just as it was, he takes a step back. He motions towards the offering, says something else, and continues to retreat backward.

Why did he do that? *Why*, just keeps looping through my head. Is it a trap? Is the meat drugged or poisoned? Either way, if I eat it in the pod and die or pass out, he still won't be able to get in. Unless of course he has a tool or something, but then he would have to know I ate the food, he'd have to see it. He can't see me. *Yet he keeps staring into the camera as if he can.*

My mind just can't compute what's going on here. I can't make any of it make any sense. It could be a trap, but then it seems like such a stupid trap. He had the food further out and he was closer, yet he didn't run for me or anything. He didn't act at all as if he was trying to catch me. As smart as he is, I bet he could have set a real trap, with a real snare, now that I think of it. Stupid, unsuspecting me would have walked right into it.

If anything, he seemed so upset I didn't take the food. If I wasn't so terrified of him I might have actually felt bad about it. And he set the food up even closer for me to take. What was the point of that? Perhaps he expects me to pause and eat the food there. That makes more sense.

I watch him, he turns around and disappears into the strand of trees. I don't feel relieved this time. This entire encounter has only left me more confused and conflicted.

The only other reason I can think of that he left the food there was as a gift. But why? Why give me water? Why feed me? What does he gain from this?

My stomach growls and twists painfully. It doesn't care why the food is there, it just wants me to take it. I push the green button. The food is so close, as soon as the wall is all the way down, I just reach out and grab it. I grab the stick then immediately stick it in my mouth. I about swoon and fall over before I grab the two fruits. I hit the button. The wall goes back up. Nothing else happens.

Food, real food. My mouth is alive with the taste and texture. My taste buds are exploding with pleasure. I had forgotten how good food could actually taste. I forgot how good it is to actually sink my teeth into something that didn't threaten to break them. I tear into the meat as if I'm an animal. *As if I'm the savage.*

When the meat is gone, I lick my fingers, sucking up every last drop of juice left. It tasted just like chicken. I then lick the stick, completely cleaning it. After placing the stick in the box, and washing it all down with a full cup of water, I wrap my blanket around me. I curl up in a ball on the floor, between the seat and dashboard. I'm full. I'm blissfully full and about to slip into a food coma.

That night I dream of him again.

***

The alien tastes so good as he kisses me. His mouth slants over my mouth, pulling back deep, lingering kisses. I can't explain the taste of him. He tastes cool and sweet, like fresh moon water and roses.

We're outside, I'm spread out naked on a bed of soft, springy grass. I feel better than I've felt in days. I feel clean and soft. My scalp isn't itching. I squirm myself against the grass. It feels wonderful to feel something else besides cold, hard metal beneath me.

His are kisses slow. He pauses to gaze lovingly at me as if he's seriously cherishing this moment. It's dark out, over his shoulder I can see the night sky. The stars twinkle and sparkle, watching us from above.

He's naked, we're touching skin to skin with nothing between us. In the blink of an eye, I go from peaceful and content to flooded with icy panic.

I try to sit up, but he senses my distress and grabs me by the face.

"Don't be afraid," he says.

My heart skips a beat. *I can understand him.* My panic increases.

"Shhh," he tries to comfort me. "You don't have to be afraid of me."

"Let me go!" I cry and I push at his hard chest. It doesn't faze him one bit.

"No," the alien says firmly. His hands tighten against my cheeks, holding me in place, forcing me to stare back at him. His eyes lock on my eyes. At first, they're a beautiful violet color. I watch in horror as that beautiful color bleeds to red.

"Let me go! Please!" I start to hit at his chest.

He frowns. His growl nearly frightens me to death, "Never. You're mine."

I grab at his hands and try to tear them from my face. "No, please, no."

"Mine," he repeats, his red eyes flashing.

I wake up with his words ringing in my ears. You're mine. Mine. He said it with such conviction. I shiver and wrap my blanket more tightly around me. As nightmares go, that's one of the worst ones I've had yet.

I don't think the food is agreeing with me… or maybe it's this forsaken planet.

CHAPTER NINE

Today, I originally planned to do some more observation. I wanted to get a better feel for the alien's routine and when would be the best time to slip off without being detected. But I can't stay in this disgusting dress another day.

It's a shame, really, I think as I pick at my hem. This pink gown of mine cost quite a large fortune. It was specifically designed and tailored for me for my birthday party. I endured months of fittings and being stabbed with pins by an overbearing team of ten designers.

Now it's filthy rags.

I remember how I fell in love with this dress of mine when I first donned it. I felt beautiful. For the first time, I felt like an actual princess and not an object to be hidden and closely guarded.

Vrillum liked this dressed. He liked how it felt when he rubbed his hands against it.

The memory makes me shudder.

I've already discarded my undergarments in the portable potty. There was no saving them. If I was more comfortable with myself, I could have taken the dress off during my time trapped in here, after all, who would see me besides the creepy purple alien? But the hopeful part of me kept it on, just in case a rescue party showed up. I wouldn't have wanted to be naked to meet them.

I hit the green button on the dashboard and the wall retracts. It's morning outside. The day is bright and for the moment, full of promise.

I look first to the strand of trees. There's no alien there. Then I scan the ground, checking for any more offerings. Thankfully, there's nothing.

I take a step out, then another. Nothing happens. I hear the familiar clicks and chirps of the local wildlife. My ears strain, ready to pick up the slightest disturbance.

I've yet to see him during the morning. Yesterday, it was what, two, three hours before he showed up? If I go now and I'm quick, I can get back before he comes back. I circle around the pod, slowly, anxiously, my eyes scanning my surroundings.

Go. I should just go. *Which way did I find water last time?* I should probably avoid that area. I think it was to my right so I point myself to the left. I do one last, thorough sweep of the area and the area I'm planning to explore. Nothing moves, nothing twitches.

You're wasting time. You're already away from the door.

Realizing how vulnerable I am has all the little hairs on my body standing on end.

If he wants to get you he's going to get you.

Father help me, I gotta get out of here before I freak myself out so much I don't chance it. I take off running while trying not to look back.

My slippers skip over the blue-green grass until I make it to the line of trees, but I have to slow and take my time as I enter the forest. I pick my way carefully over the branches, rocks, and uneven ground. If I would have known I would be roughing it, I would have worn better shoes.

If I would have known this was going to happen, I would have never gone up in Vrillum's ship.

The forest is quiet, eerily quiet, and the deeper I go, the cooler it gets. I actually find myself shivering. I wrap my arms around myself and sniff the air. I don't think I'll be able to find water with my nose this time. The forest is misty, the air thick with moisture. I'll have to keep an ear out for moving water or hope I just stumble across it like last time.

My slippers are taking a serious beating. The ground is soft and mud clings to my soles. The deeper I go, the more my feet sink. The canopy overhead thickens. The tree branches seemingly begin to intertwine with each other. Leaves on top of leaves. It grows darker and darker. Between the lack of light and the mist, it feels entirely too creepy for my liking. I decide to turn around and make my way back the way I came.

Maybe I should have marked the way I came.

I was hoping to get lucky again, to stumble across water quickly. The chance I could get myself lost never even crossed my mind. At first, I have my own tracks to follow, my footprints left in the mud. But as I walk out, and the ground hardens, my footsteps disappear and I'm left just to guess.

If only I could have walked in a straight line, I wouldn't need to worry, but with so many trees in the way, and so many obstacles that could trip me, I picked my way around, choosing the easiest paths. Now, I try to choose the easiest path back, but I have an uneasy feeling. Things don't quite look the same. And after walking for some time, I realize I'm lost.

The trees should be thinning out, there should be more light, but it's remained just as dark. I stop and try to get my bearings. I spin in a slow circle, looking for something that seems familiar. All I see is trees and more trees, mist, and more mist.

Just as I'm about to choose a new direction, the path that seems the least misty, I hear the cracking sound of a branch snapping, breaking the eerie silence.

My heart flutters. I spin around, but I don't see anything. I don't feel comfortable. My heart is racing a mile a minute. There're too many dark, misty spots where something could be hiding. Suddenly I feel like I'm being watched. *It's probably the space demon.*

The urge to flee is almost overwhelming. I decide to stick with my first choice and head down the least misty way. I make it about a dozen feet when I hear another branch snapping behind me. *That's not a coincidence.*

I cast a fearful glance over my shoulder, but it's hard to look back and keep moving forward. There's too much I have to watch out for. My toe snags on a branch and I go down on one knee. I scramble back upright and rush forward. I've learned my lesson.

I focus on the ground and my own feet.

Another branch snaps behind me and then another. Whatever is behind me is rushing to catch up with me.

Please let it be a bunny or something, please. I wish I could run. I wish I knew just where the heck I was going. As I keep moving forward, the mist continues to thin. I make it another dozen feet and thankfully the thing behind me hasn't caught up to me yet.

Rushing, I keep rushing. I see the trees thinning out in front of me. It's hope. I surge onward. The going gets easier and easier. There're less trees around, less stuff on the ground to trip me up. Less stuff to snag my dress on.

The trees spread, yards grow between them. The mist dissipates. Everything is lit up by the morning sun. The next thing I know I actually am running. I'm running and running, my shredded gown fluttering behind me. I'm running as if I actually have a chance.

I make it, somehow I make it. I reach a clearing. There're several rocks and a small river of running water. I run up to the biggest rock and climb up on it. I whip around, expecting to finally see whatever it is that's chasing me. There's nothing there.

Was I just imagining it? Freaking myself out?

My eyes comb the trees, the ground, and even the sky. I could have sworn I was being chased, that something was trying to catch me. Why would it stop? Maybe it gave up awhile back?

Well, whatever it is, I conclude, it's not the alien. I have a feeling that if it was him chasing me, he would have caught me. Or, even if he didn't catch me, he wouldn't just stop. Hopefully, I was just running from my own twisted imagination.

I hop off the rock and start to pace around. My heart is still racing and I have to give it time to slow. After a couple of minutes, I bend over. I start to retch. As the panic fades away, I feel the sickness. My breathing is loud and uneven. I pushed myself too hard and too fast, now I'm paying for it.

I didn't eat breakfast before I left so all I end up getting out is a lot of spit. My stomach eventually settles. I wipe my mouth off with the back of my hand.

Okay, I found water, yay! But now I'm seriously lost. I look up at the sun's position in the sky and I think at least an hour has passed. Air in the nose and out the mouth. I think I'm done getting sick.

I've been gone longer than I would have liked. This whole plan of mine has really gone to shit. If the alien checks on the pod, he'll know I'm not there, what with the wall being down and all. He'll have full access to the pod and everything in it. Or he'll come looking for me. I don't know which is worse.

I walk over to the water and gaze into it. It's crystal clear, so clear I can see the muddy bottom. I bend over and dip my hand in the water. It's not exactly cold, but it's not exactly warm. A cool bath is better than no bath at all.

I have yet to hear another branch breaking and so far nothing has come upon me. Yet, I feel full of dread. I feel like I've gotten myself into quite a mess, and I'm not sure if this time I can get myself out of it.

I lower myself down to the ground, cross my legs and just sit and listen. It's peaceful, even relaxing here. The quiet is filled only with the sounds of the water flowing and splashing against the rocks.

If only an hour has passed, there is still hope left, I reassure myself. The alien may not check on the pod for several hours. Perhaps I can still take a bath and get back. The feeling of dread eases a bit. The thought of finally rinsing the layers of yuck off my skin lifts my spirits.

I slide off my slippers. They are beyond ruined, torn and caked with a mud that will never come off. I look down to my dress. I'm not even sure it's still a dress. It's ripped and shredded. It's truly rags now, hanging on only by a few expensive threads.

I set the slippers down to my left, uncross my legs, point my toes and test the water again. It's still tepid. I would prefer it warm, but I'll take what I can get. I let my legs go and watch as they drop down beneath the rippling surface. My reflection is there, wavering. I avoid looking at it by sliding the rest of my body in.

The water feels amazing. My feet touch the muddy bottom. I sink down until my shoulders are covered. As the water settles, I catch another glimpse of my reflection so I close my eyes and hold my breath. I sink all the way down until the water is covering my head.

I hold myself under the water until my lungs threaten to burst. Then I surface, gasping for air, only to drop back down when I've caught my breath. Under the water, I run my hands along my body, rubbing off the grime the best that I can. Frustratingly, the rags I'm still wearing serve only get in my way. I wish I was brave enough to remove them.

I rub my skin until it's tender and pink. Then I scrub at my scalp, scratching and scraping, trying to get rid of the itch. *If only I had soap*, I think wistfully as I work on my hair. Water can only do so much, it's going to take some actual industrial strength soap, hot water, and a lot more scrubbing before I'll ever truly feel clean again.

All the scrubbing and scratching saps up the last of my energy so I regretfully pull myself out onto the bank. I'm sopping wet and have nothing to dry off with. My rags are heavy and dripping streams. I grab up handfuls and wring them out, but it doesn't help much. I need to dry off a bit before I set out to find my way back. The forest is cold and misty. If I don't warm up I'll catch my death before I ever make it back.

The big rock seems like the best place to rest and dry myself out so I climb back up on it and spread myself out. I lay back with my hands under my head.

The rock is warm beneath me. Even though it's hard, its way more comfortable than the cold floor I've been sleeping on. The rock also has a direct beam of sunlight. I soak up the warmth of the sun but still I start shivering.

It's my dress. My dress is keeping me cold. The sun just can't penetrate it.

So far paranoia has kept me from removing my dress. My teeth start to chatter, however, and the choice is taken right out of my hands. I have to remove my dress before I shiver myself sick.

I sit up and work the rags down. The way it clings, it feels more like I'm peeling off a layer of skin. Once the rags are off, I wring the whole thing out and spread it out on the side of the rock. For now it clings to the rock. When it dries off, it will probably slip off and fall to the ground.

Fully nude now, the sun touches and warms every exposed inch of my flesh. I gather up my hair in my hands and twist it, ringing the water out just as I did with my dress. Once my hair is only damp, I lean back with a sigh of contentment on my lips. I fan my hair out on the rock, so it will dry, and try to relax as the heat sinks in.

Eventually, I start to drift off. Maybe it's because of the nightmare or maybe it's because I'm naked, but soon my thoughts start to drift towards the alien.

In my dreams, he wants to kiss me and call me his. In reality, I don't know what to make of him. I must do my best not to confuse my dreams with reality. I must not let my guard drop and let him in.

Why did he bring me food and water? Why help me? I'm pretty sure none of it was poisoned. He didn't seem to gain anything by it unless his purpose is to gain my trust so I'm less guarded around him. Shit. Maybe he did it so I'd be brave enough to try something reckless, something like this.

I'm so stupid. Stupid got me into this mess.

It's not even the whole lost in the woods thing I've got going on. My stupidity is what got me marooned on this planet to begin with. I trusted my stepbrother, Vrillum. I let him convince me that I should have one last hurrah before my Father officially announced my engagement. I let him sweet talk me into believing one just hasn't lived until they've been off the planet.

This isn't living, this is surviving, and I'm doing a damn poor job at it.

CHAPTER TEN

A twig snaps and my eyes pop open in alarm.
I'm not sure how long I let myself get lost in
thought, but I'm pretty sure it was for too long. I sit
up and grab up my dress. I clutch it to my chest as
my eyes search for the source of the sound.

Another twig snaps and I catch a glimpse of
something small and furry darting around a tree.

My shoulders slump and I release the tension
that was building up in a long, relieved breath. It's
just a bunny or some other harmless creature.
Nothing to be afraid of. Time to gather up my stuff,
though, and get out of here. *Before something bigger
and badder shows up.*

Another twig snaps. I slide off the side of the
rock. The furry creature darts out from behind the
tree. We stare at each other, ten feet or so between
us. It's small, brown and reminds me of a squirrel.
Except where I come from squirrels don't have big,
black eyes or long, razor sharp claws.

Where I come from, squirrels also tend to be skittish around people, and rarely get close to them. This little creature has no fear of me. It runs straight for me and stops only inches from my bare feet. It makes a chirping sound and it's large, black eyes peer up at me. Its large gleaming eyes make it oh so cute. It reminds me of one of the forest creatures in the cartoons I watched growing up.

"Hello there, little guy," I say softly.

The little creature makes another chirping noise. Is it trying to communicate with me?

"Were you what was chasing me?"

The creature only blinks.

"Well, I gotta get going... have fun..."

The little animal is adorable, but I know better than to reach out to touch it or to try to pick it up. It's a wild animal and the last thing I need to deal with is a scratch or some kind of alien rabies. I have all my shots, but I'm not vaccinated for the stuff on this planet. I hope it doesn't follow me back to the pod.

I take a step to the side and look up. There's a loud commotion off in the distance that draws my attention. I lift my foot as if to take another step but stop dead in my tracks. Ice floods my veins. It's hard to breathe. My heart thunders behind my ribs.

About fifty yards or so is the big purple alien and he's running. He's heading straight for me.

"Shit," I curse.

The little animal hisses and bares its fangs. It darts forward and tries to take a bite out of my foot. I yank my foot back just in time and dance away from it.

Just what I needed.

I scramble backwards, but the only place to go is to the water or to the left. I mean to go to the left, but the little animal comes after me again.

"Hey!" I yelled at it, "Shoo! Bugger off!"

I kick at it and it retreats back.

I side step to the left and stop short. Another fuzzy creature pops its head out from behind a tree and chirps.

"I will stomp you if you don't back off!" I warn the little animals, but they ignore me. They're chirping at each other and I bet, I just bet they're hashing out a plan.

The water it is. I hope the little buggers can't swim. I start to ease myself back. The alien is gaining ground. He's going to catch me if I don't do something quick.

Something chirps behind me.

I cast a glance over my shoulder and sure enough, on the other side of the water is another fuzzy creature with fangs.

What do I do now?

The fuzzball in front of me rushes forward while its buddy comes at me from the left. I kick out at the one in front of me and swing my dress at the one to my left. They both back off of me for a moment then they start to circle around me.

Dammit, why do they have to be so intelligent and nasty?

I'd have to spin to keep my eyes on them, but then I remember I've taken my eyes off the alien. He should have reached me by now. My eyes flick away for just a moment and one of the creatures shrieks. I look down in confusion. It's gone.

Where did it go?

I look to the other creature. It shrieks as well as a rock smashes into it and sends its little body flying away from me. I look up and there the purple alien is, five yards away from me with another rock poised and ready in his hand.

"Thank you!" I call out and take off running to the left.

The forest erupts with chirps. Little heads with large black eyes and snarling fangs pop out from everywhere. I dig my heels in the dirt and come to a screeching halt.

There's so many... Where did they all come from? I can't even...

I turn right back around and start running towards the alien.

"Help!" I scream.

I think I'll take my chances with him.

The alien drops the rock and raises his fists in the air. He reminds me of a massive purple gorilla as all the muscles in his body seemingly flex and he lets out a blood-curdling roar.

It feels as if everything inside me just drops. My bottom fell out. He rushes forward and my life flashes before my eyes. This is it. I'm so dead.

I'm too scared to even care.

The alien rushes past me. I could have sworn he was going to barrel right through me, but he swerves and gives me a wide berth.

I hear the carnage behind me before I actually see it. The sounds of the creatures getting hurt is disturbing. I know they're mean, nasty little things that would have eaten me but their sounds of pain are too high pitched. They sound like puppies getting kicked. It's hard on the soul.

Slowly, I spin around, afraid of what I'm going to find. But something inside me has to see what is going on. I have to know.

I clutch my dress to my chest and shiver. It's still wet and cold.

The alien is fighting dozens of the fuzzy creatures. He's covered in their blood. They launch at him from the ground and even from above. There's so many of them. The alien's fists don't slow. Most of the creatures get punched or kicked, but a lucky few get grabbed. If he doesn't send them rocketing through the air, to splatter against a tree, he rips off their little heads. He's completely berserk.

I watch in fascinated horror as he dispatches each one until there's nothing left but carnage.

Turning to face me, he's huffing loudly, with his shoulders hunched forward. We stare at each other. Me in terror, him coming down from his rage. His red eyes are glowing so bright the light begins to sting my eyes.

Something makes a sound to his right. He roars and stomps over to dispatch it. I turn and flee for my life.

We really need to stop meeting like this.

I make it a few yards before I hear him crashing through the forest behind me. It's no mere snapping of twigs. It sounds as if the very forest is coming down around me. He's a tornado of destruction and I'm directly in his path.

Don't look back. Don't look back.

I'm running back into the dark, misty depths. Back into the cold labyrinth of trees. I have a little head start but a lot of good it does me as I stumble over the unending sea of fallen twigs and branches. I'm so not cut out for this. Maybe if I was smarter, faster, or stronger I'd actually have a chance.

But I'm a princess. A princess who has been sheltered and protected, a princess who's never had to worry about the dangers that exist beyond the safe little bubble of her home.

I feel danger coming up behind me and it's fast.

The alien's hands grab me by the hips. One second I'm running, the next he's lifting me up and my feet leave the ground. I scream as his thick arms wrap around me. They're as tight and strong as two boa constrictors. They squeeze around me in an unbreakable hold.

Knowing he's stronger and more powerful doesn't keep me from struggling. I scream and kick at his shins. He squeezes me harder. One beefy arm comes up to trap my arms. I lose my grip on my dress. I cry out in anguish as it falls to the ground.

He says something in his alien tongue. Again, to me it sounds only like coughs and grunts instead of actual words.

I don't have a lot of energy left. My kicks slow, growing feeble. I feel tears of defeat stinging my eyes.

Why keep fighting? I'm so tired of fighting. I'm so tired of it all.

He's stronger, faster, and meaner. It was only a matter a time before he caught me. Only a matter of time until it came to this. I've been delaying the inevitable and making myself miserable in the process.

I give up.

***

"Please just make it quick." I clench my eyes tightly together and brace myself for the pain to come. Even a quick death is probably going to hurt like a mother.

The alien doesn't say anything, but I feel him snort against the back of my neck. His arms start to loosen and then he's turning my body until I'm facing him. I can't help but peek my eyes open.

He looks every bit the demon. I'm surprised there are not two horns sprouting from his head. He is truly the stuff of nightmares. I bet he's related to the thing I always feared was hiding under my bed. And it's not even his red eyes though they certainly don't hurt. It's his massive bulging purple body. And it's the fearsome, I'm going to eat you after I break you look on his face.

I squeeze my eyes shut again. I rather not see what's going to come. My arms fall limply to my sides. They ache and feel numb from where he was cutting off my circulation.

He speaks again. It's a grating growl that scrapes against my ears. I shake my head to rid myself of the sound.

He snorts. I begin to tremble. I don't know how much more I can take of this. My bravery is fading fast. If he keeps me here, waiting, dreading, I'm seriously going to break down.

"Please, just get it over with, please," I beg with a whisper.

His fingers tighten once more, digging painfully into my arms. He shakes me as if he's angry. I cry out. *This is it. This is where I end.* He immediately stops shaking me yet my body continues to tremble.

I never thought I would go out like this, killed on some backwoods planet by a monster from the dark. Up until crashing here, I never even gave death much thought. There were so many other people always protecting me and looking out for me, I didn't have to do it for myself. I just let them do it.

The demon pulls me into him. He's so hard, it's as if his chest is carved from stone. His hands slide down my arms, I wince as my skin tingles.

His hands go behind me and begin to rub against my back. My eyes fly open in shock.

At first, all I see is just lots of purple skin. Then my eyes slide up, over his bulging pecs and up his ridiculously thick neck, until reaching his face. He's looking down at me, still intense and glowing, but the way he's touching my back is soft. For a moment, it actually feels like he's trying to comfort me or something. But no, that couldn't be....

A chirp sounds behind him and I watch his face darken, consumed by red. Before I can completely process what's happening, he hauls me up and throws me over his shoulder.

I'm upside down now with the blood rushing to my head. He takes off running through the woods. My naked butt bounces in the air.

"No, my dress!" I cry out as I spot it in a little pink pile on the ground that grows smaller and smaller.

I don't even know why I did it. I mean, I know I'm not going to need my dress now with what's going to happen to me but seeing it left behind, left to rot, just tears at my heart. It's all I have left, and even though I'm going to die in some horrific way and have no real need of it, I want it. *I want my last piece of home.*

The alien doesn't stop, if anything, his pace quickens. He does, however, give me a small pat on the butt. I burst into tears.

Just when I think the situation can't get any worse, it does. Over and over again, I think I've hit bottom but the hole keeps getting deeper and deeper. I can't even have the small dignity of a quick death. The entire thing has to be dragged out. Why did I even give up?

I hate crying, I just hate it. I hate it because it makes me feel weak and pathetic. I hate it because it makes my skin all blotchy and reddens my nose.

I'm dripping tears and snot all over his back. It's so nasty and gross.

He runs and runs, his pace never slowing. The trees whip past in one long blur. Occasionally I hear a chirp.

I want to stop crying so I try my best to focus on something else. Chin up, princess. *You're a princess after all.*

I feel helpless being naked and thrown over his shoulder. Like I'm just a piece of meat. Like I'm nothing more than hauled away flesh and bone.

I've been put on display before. Dressed up and paraded before an entire populace as a living, breathing symbol. All my life I've been judged by how I look, who I talk to, what I do, and what I wear. I learned fast that my needs, my wants, my desires were of no interest to anyone else. I have a purpose, a single duty to serve my people and beyond that nothing else really matters. But I still had my clothes.

This is humiliating. This goes far beyond degrading. I can't stop feeling sorry for myself.

My butt is in the air, there's nothing I can do to change it. I squirm and twist, but it gets me nowhere. He has one arm across the back of my legs while his other hand rests on the small of my back. There's a weight of possession to the way he carries me. And I can't help but notice how his fingers tend to squeeze, even if it's just a little.

I have no dignity left. I feel every bit like a piece of meat. He's such a monster, he's probably completely oblivious. He probably doesn't even care.

So I hit him. I'm crazy, I know it, completely wacko, but what do I have to lose? He's already going to hurt me. I just feel the strongest urge to hurt him and make him pay for what he's doing.

My fists pound into his back. They may be tiny,
but they're powered by anger. I hate him. I hate
him so much.

"I hate your guts!" I cry out and give him a one-
two.

I hate that not only has he tormented me since I
crashed here but now he's reduced me to this. He's
pushed me into giving up.

I hit and hit but quickly tire. I can no longer
muscle up the energy to punch his back, but I'm still
so mad. If anything, he's complete lack of response
to what I'm doing is even more infuriating. I want
him to acknowledge my hatred. I want him to be at
the very least inconvenienced by it.

I get the bright idea to grab onto his pants. I'm
going to give him the biggest, most uncomfortable
wedgie an alien can get.

Where did he get the pants from?

The first time we "met", if you can even call it
that, he was completely naked. I remember because
I will never forget that what he has dangling
between his legs is scary huge. Did he steal them off
of someone else? That someone would have to be
just as big as him… I don't even want to think about
it. Let's not go there.

I grab and yank with all the strength I have left.

I hear a smack then feel a searing white hot pain
bloom on my butt.

Did he just spank me?

I yank again and sure enough I hear the snap as his hand connects. At first my left cheek stings then the stinging sensation melts into something warm.

His pace starts to slow and I don't feel so brave anymore. I quickly release his pants and just let my hands hang down. I'm all saggy and innocent now.

He comes to a complete stop. I wait with bated breath, I wait for him to enact some more retribution. Or just put an end to this entire ordeal.

Instead, I hear some beeping then the hiss of air pressure being released.

Uh, what's going on?

I can't see anything hanging upside down. I try to twist, but I'm tired and too heavy, it's too hard to move. He's extra wide, the only way I'll be able to see around him is if I develop x-ray vision.

I know it's not the pod, it can't be, the only buttons are on the inside and I would recognize that floor. I'd recognize the smell. That means…he's taken me to another ship. *But whose?*

CHAPTER ELEVEN

The alien carries me across the threshold of a ship. The dirt transforms into a black rubber type of floor. He jostles me and I hear more beeping. A door rises from the floor before my eyes, sealing us in. There's no symbols or paint on the door to give me the slightest clue of what kind of ship I'm in. It's just generic spaceship gray, as are all these walls surrounding it.

I'm trapped. The thought makes me anxious at first, but I remind myself that it doesn't really matter because he's going to kill me anyway. But what if he has something else planned?

I so don't want to think too much about that.

He moves forward. My eyes start to blur as I watch the black rubber floor roll past. *Just how big is this ship anyway?* He turns a corner and keeps on going. I'm considering giving him another wedgie when he suddenly he stops.

There's more jostling, more beeping. I hear the release as a door slides into the floor. He carries me over the threshold, walks ten more steps and then drops me down on something soft.

I bounce. My eyes cross as my world is flipped upright. It takes me a minute to get my bearings. The blood rushes back down from my head.

Everything begins to focus. I rub my fingers across the soft thing he put me on. *It can't be, can it?* I look behind me, then all around me. Finally, I look back at him.

He set me down on a bed. A massive bed. No doubt it's his bed. *Am I about to suffer a fate worse than death?*

I scramble backwards, putting as much distance between me and him that I possibly can. I push up against the headboard. I'm still naked.

I bring my knees up to my chest and wrap my arms around them. Then I glare angrily at him.

He stands at the foot of the bed, impossibly imposing. His lips are pulled down into a frown and his red eyes are burning into me.

"I will fight you!" I warn him.

And I will. I will fight him if he tries to force himself on me, I will literally fight him to the death. Had I known he wasn't going to kill me, had I known he would be carrying me to a secret spaceship only to throw me on a bed, I would have fought him back in the forest with everything I had.

He snorts loudly. *Was that derision?*

"You might as well just kill me already," I try to convince him. "I'm more trouble than I'm worth."

He tips back his head and laughs. His chest rumbles, his massive hands hit his massive thighs. I'm seriously disturbed by it. *Is he laughing because he agrees with me?*

"How can you understand me but I can't understand you?" I ask and he suddenly stops laughing.

His eyes narrow at me and if I could disappear, I would. Then he speaks. It's slow but still very guttural and growly.

"I have no idea what you just said."

He slaps the side of his head then speaks again. He's speaking dog for all I know.

"Still no clue."

He comes around the bed. I scramble backward, my heart racing with panic.

"If you mean to force yourself on me, I will fight you! I mean it!"

He reaches for me, I jerk backward and tumble off the bed. For something so big, he sure does move fast. He comes across the bed and looms above me. I shriek and try to get away as he comes down to the floor.

"Don't you dare!" I scream at him and scoot back

He crawls forward. My head is throbbing from where I landed on it. The look on his face is so predatory. There's an unmistakable hunger in the way he's looking at me.

He's going to eat me up.

He keeps coming closer and I can't go anywhere else. I'm trapped in the corner. He comes up to my toes and then reaches for me.

I close my eyes and flinch. "Please...."

He grabs my hand. I try to pull it back. His fingers tighten, they're so warm...

The alien speaks slowly, softly. I still can't understand what he's saying, but it sounds so different compared to how he was speaking before. It sounds like he's trying to reassure me.

Something brushes across my knuckles and I feel an intense jolt of sensation. *Huh?*

I peek my eyes open and he does it again. He brushes his lips across my knuckles. Again, there's a jolt and then something inside me clenches.

"I still don't understand," I cry and the tears start coming. *Why is he kissing me? Am I having a perverted dream again?*

He speaks again, softly and slowly, and strangely I find a bit of comfort in it.

"Are you going to hurt me?" I ask. I feel my nose about to drip so I wipe it with the back of my other hand.

The alien answers softly. For all I know he's telling me he's going to rip me apart and wear my skin. It's the tone that's reassuring. The tone that brings my heart rate back down and lulls me into a momentary break from the panic.

Surely if he meant to kill me or eat me, he wouldn't go through all this trouble… he wouldn't be crouched in front of me, holding my hand? He's so big. All he has to do is wrap those thick fingers of his around my neck and it's lights out. I have no weapons, I have no means to defend myself. He can easily take what he wants from me and there's nothing I can do about it. Yet, that's not what he's doing.

We stare at each other. I don't know what to make of him. In my mind, he's one giant contradiction. I wish I could understand him.

"Where I come from, we nod our heads for yes and shake our heads for no."

He nods his head.

"So you are going to hurt me?!" I cry out, thinking he's answering my question.

He's quick to frown and shake his head.

"You're not going to hurt me?"

He nods his head fast.

"Why are you doing this?"

He just stares at me.

Oh, right. Yes or no questions only.

"Are you going to kill me?"

He shakes his head again.

"May I have some clothes?"

He just stares at me again, and I wonder if he didn't understand the question or something. Finally, he nods his head.

"May I have my hand back?" My fingers are beginning to tingle.

He looks down at my hand and sighs deeply. He let's go as if he's reluctant to do so.

I flex my fingers then pull my hand back. "Thank you."

We fall into silence. He holds himself very still. I try to think of some yes or no questions that will give me an idea of what he intends or expects.

"When you rolled my pod, I thought you were trying to kill me."

His eyebrows twitch. Funny, because of his glowing red eyes, I never really noticed them until now. They're thick, black, and very expressive. I look closer at the rest of his face. For a purple guy with evil eyes, he's actually not that bad looking. He has a fine nose and full lips. His forehead is broad and his chin is strong, just like the rest of him.

He shakes his head.

"Were you trying to hurt me?"

He shakes his head again and it's my turn to frown.

"Does this ship work?"

He shakes his head.

"Dammit."

He nods.

I smile for a second, his eyes flash. I bite my lip to hide my smile. What was that?

I look away. I'm so out of sorts. "May I have some clothes now?"

Maybe it's because he seems to be respecting me and because he's answering my questions, but I don't quite feel like my life is in danger now. The fact that he hasn't tried to touch me again certainly helps. Though, something weird seems to be happening between us, and I'm not entirely comfortable or sure where it's leading. The friction has changed. *Or maybe it's always been there but because you were so afraid you didn't notice it.* Or more like I've been stuck alone, in a pod for however many days now with no one to talk to and he's the first... thing I've been able to communicate with.

Regardless, I feel exhaustion starting to creep in. It's been a long day, too much has happened. There's been too much thinking done and there's still too much to figure out. If I can get some clothes on, maybe he'll let me use the bed and rest. Alone.

He reaches for me and I can't help but flinch and pull back. I'm not sure if I do it because I'm still afraid he'll hurt me or I'm afraid I'll feel that jolt.

He seems offended. He gives a sharp nod of his head and pushes himself up to his feet.

I hope I didn't piss him off. *I'll have to be more careful not to do that.* Piss him off, that is.

He walks over to the wall by the door and I notice there's a panel with some buttons. He pushes a button and part of the wall behind him disappears, revealing a closet. He looks over the contents of the closet carefully, then he grabs something black and pushes the button to close the closet door.

He strides back over to me and then extends the black fabric in offering.

"Thank you," I tell him as I accept it.

He stares at me.

I twirl my finger in the air telling him, "Will you please turn around?"

Yeah, he's already seen all of me naked and as I am, I'm not hiding much. But it's the principle that counts. He needs to know and understand I don't feel comfortable being naked in front of him.

He points to me, then he points to the bed.

I have to keep myself calm when I ask, "You want me to sleep there?" Because I'm afraid he means or wants something else.

He nods. *Whew.*

"I want to sleep alone," I make clear.

He frowns. I was afraid of that.

If he pushes the issue, will I be able to sleep in a bed with him? I think not.

"You can have the bed, then. I'll sleep on the floor."

He angrily shakes his head.

"So you'll let me sleep in the bed? Alone?"

Begrudgingly he nods his head.

I smile and tell him, "Thank you!"

He seems pleased by this because he smiles back.

"May I have some privacy now?"

The smile fades away and he gives me a long, heated stare. My body reacts involuntarily as his red, glowing eyes roam over me, they're like two burning coals, warming me with their touch.

It's over almost as quickly as it began. He tears his eyes away from me, spins on his heel and stomps over the threshold. He pushes the button and I stare at him as the door rises from the floor until I can't see anymore.

I hear him stomping down the hall. My shoulders slump. I'm overcome with exhaustion.

What just happened? Did I imagine all of it? I think things were easier when I thought he wanted to eat me. What am I now? A pet?

CHAPTER TWELVE

I haven't slept in a bed for days. There's a massive soft bed in front of me and I couldn't take advantage of it. I ended up falling asleep huddled in my little corner on the floor.

When I wake, I've got a bad creak in my neck. My face feels puffy and my eyes still burn as if I'm tired. I think I slept and I think I'm awake now. It's hard to be sure, though, because being here feels so weird. *Is this a dream?*

From my vantage point on the floor, I'm still alone. Shakily I get to my feet and begin to poke around. I touch everything. I touch the bed, running my fingers across the silky sheets. I touch the walls, hoping to discover the grooves of other hidden doors. It feels good just to walk around, to have space to explore.

I walk over to the panel of buttons on the wall. Dammit, all the buttons are the same color. It would be so much easier if there was a way to tell them apart.

I hesitate for a moment and then push a button, thinking perhaps it was the button he pushed last night to open the closet door. Nothing happens so I try another button. Then another.

Perhaps he disabled it somehow?

I hear his heavy footsteps stomping from somewhere on the other side of the door. *Crap.* I run over to the bed and sit down. I smooth the black shirt over my thighs and try to look natural.

The alien speaks something and then the door drops down, sinking into the floor. *Ah, he switched it to voice recognition.* Given how crude his language is, it will be a miracle if I can get the commands figured out.

He steps into the room and stops right inside the door. The room fills with tension as our eyes meet and we stare at each other.

I don't know what to expect. Is he going to be as soft and comforting as he tried to be last night? Or is he going to be the scary monster that rolled my pod into the forest?

I hold my breath and try to keep myself from being consumed by panic. Freaking out might make things worse. I look up from his eyes and focus on his eyebrows. *That's better.*

The alien says something slow and soft.

I sigh, "I don't understand."

I watch his brow furrow.

He walks towards me. It takes every ounce of control I have to keep from recoiling as he walks right into my personal bubble. He reaches out and I can't help but flinch, I still expect him to hurt me. He grabs my hand instead. He lifts my hand and brushes his lips across my knuckles, just like last night. I feel that jolt, the one that shocks my core.

I just have to ask, "Are you like electrified or something?"

I've had my hand kissed before, but it never felt like this. And the way my toes just want to curl, I know that jolt wasn't simple static.

His lips curve into a smirk as if he's amused by my question and he shakes his head.

I narrow my eyes at him as if I don't believe him, and he brushes his lips across my knuckles again.

"Stop that!" I gasp and try to pull back my hand.

He doesn't give it back. Instead, he uses it as leverage to pull me to my feet. My chest tightens, I can't breathe. He pulls me closer and I'm afraid, so afraid. But I'm not afraid he's going to hurt me or even kill me. I'm afraid he's going to kiss me.

And I'm afraid I'm going to like it.

His face grows bigger and bigger. His eyes are half-lidded. He's going in for the kiss, I just know it. I turn my face away at the last moment and feel his warm sigh against my hair.

He pulls back so quick, I have to wonder if I was reading too much into his intentions. By the hand, he pulls me forward and leads me out to the hall. He walks fast, so fast, I find myself jogging to keep up.

He was trying to kiss me, wasn't he? Or did I totally just read that wrong and offend him?

We turn a corner, rush down a hallway, then turn another corner.

Where are we going? Is he going to throw me out?

Would I be upset if he did?

"Please slow down!" I huff out as he pulls me around yet another corner. It feels like we could have made a complete square by now.

The alien's pace immediately slows. His legs are so long, however, that I still have to take two steps for his each one.

"Thank you," I say breathlessly.

He squeezes my hand. Another thrilling jolt shoots up my arm.

He leads me down another hall, around another corner, and finally into a room. With all the benches and tables, I assume it's a mess hall. The room looks like it could easily seat a hundred people if they're sized like me. If they're sized like him, it's looking more like fifty.

In the back corner, near an open door that I assume leads to a kitchen area, is a table already set with plates and food. My tummy rumbles loudly and my cheeks warm with embarrassment. I didn't even realize I was hungry until now but as the smell wafts towards me, my mouth waters and my stomach aches.

The alien leads me towards the table. I have eyes only for the food when he lets go of my hand. I sit down on the bench, pull up the plate and start digging in. As I pick up the skewered meat, the very same juicy delicious meat he left for me at my pod, I'm vaguely aware that he takes the bench across from me.

I tear into the meat and its juices drip all over my fingers. I'm so ravenous, I barely even chew it. It's tear, swallow, repeat. Once all the meat is devoured and I'm done gnawing on the stick, I go about cleaning my fingers by licking them. I just can't get enough. That's when I feel the hairs on the back of my neck stand on end.

I peek up and the purple guy is staring at me so intensely, his eyes focused on my mouth and my fingers, I feel incredibly self-conscious.

"I'm sorry!" I apologize. I didn't even ask him if I could have the food. I was so hungry I just ate it…

He just shakes his head and then I notice he has a plate in front of him. He picks up the skewer from his plate and extends it in offering.

I bite my lip. I don't want to be rude and refuse his gift, and I certainly don't want to anger him. But I also feel guilty by eating his food. Who knows how much food he has on hand?

"Thank you, but you should eat it." *Looks like your bulging muscles need it.*

He shakes his head again and jabs the skewer at me.

My stomach rumbles. "Well, if you insist…"

I reach out and pluck the skewer from his hand. Then I dig in. This time, when I'm finished, I actually take a moment to consider wiping my hands off on something. But there are no napkins and the shirt I'm wearing is the first clean thing I've had to wear in days, I really don't want to sully it. So I lick my fingers clean again.

He stares at me, unabashedly while I do it. His eyes are red hot as my fingers slide in and out of my mouth. I don't know how I feel about his attention. I have so many conflicting emotions warring inside me. Part of me is still frightened of him. I've been afraid of him for weeks. I may very well have the wrong impression, but he is so damn scary looking, it's hard not to be afraid. Yet another part of me is excited. I don't know what is wrong with that part of me. It's excited that he's giving me his attention, excited that he's interested in me. It wants to play with the fire.

The thing I know for sure is that I need him and I need him to want to help me. Whatever happened before, I need to just get over it. He's given me food, protection, and shelter. That speaks more than actual words ever could. I need to focus on staying in his good graces so he continues providing. I have a feeling that I'm going to need his help if I want to get off this rock.

Yet, I do need to be careful he doesn't get the wrong impression. His eyes are getting that heavy, half-lidded look to them again, and he's leaning over the table now as if he wants to get closer to me. I promptly pull my fingers from my lips and drop my wet hand to my lap. Yuck.

He frowns and leans back.

I decide to change the subject by asking, "Did your ship crash here?"

He nods his head and picks up a fruit from his plate. The fruit is small, round, and dark blue.

It's my turn to watch him as he peels the skin off the fruit. His white teeth flash as he lifts it to his mouth and takes a big bite out of it.

"Do any of the communication systems on the ship still function?"

He finishes eating the fruit before answering me. It only takes two more bites and he gives me another shake of his head. A little bit of juice glistens at the corners of his lips. His tongue appears and I'm taken aback. It's so dark purple it's almost black, just like his hair. So dark it doesn't appear to have any color, but in the right light, highlights of purple are revealed. The color reminds me of the black roses that grow back home, in my father's garden.

"Have you been here for a long time?"

He appears to think before answering with a nod of his head. He grabs up another fruit and begins to peel it.

"Have you been alone?"

Something flashes across his face. I can't tell if it's pain or anger. He nods.

"I'm sorry. It must be rough."

He's motionless.

Okay, time to change the subject.

"I think we got started on the wrong foot." I stick out my hand. "I'm Princess Ameia."

He stares at my hand so long, I think I'm going to have to explain shaking hands to him.

I'm completely flabbergasted when he growls out, "Ameia."

"Yes!" I exclaim, just happy to hear my name spoken by someone else. "And you are?"

My hand is still hovering in the air when he grunts something I can't understand.

"I'm sorry," I frown, "I didn't quite catch that."

He grunts again, but it feels hopeless.

I sigh, shake my head, and start to pull my hand back. His hand flies out and he grabs me. I gasp as it feels like my hand was just zapped by his hand. My arm jerks and I try to pull my hand back.

He clutches my fingers and slowly growls.

All I can do is apologize again, "I'm sorry, I just don't understand."

He looks frustrated and smacks the side of his head. *Perhaps it's some weird compulsion he has when he doesn't get what he wants?* I've seen children do something similar when they're frustrated.

"Perhaps you'll allow me to use a nickname for you?" I ask, hoping to fix the situation.

He leans his head to the side and moves it as if he's trying to shake water out of it. As far as I can tell, nothing comes out. He frowns, straightens, and finally nods at me in agreement.

I think for a moment. The last thing I want to do is offend him, but the first words that pop in my head are words like big, scary, demon, alien. I doubt he'll take kindly to any of those. I could use red, black, or guy. But they don't seem right either. Certainly not flattering. Whatever his name is, I'm sure it's something that strikes fear in the hearts of his enemies Killer, Shredder, or, Fluffy

"How about I call you Friend?"

Friend without benefits.

His thick brows furrow and he shakes his head.

"You don't like that?"

He shakes his head again.

I frown. I'm not sure I like where this is going.

"We're not friends?"

He shakes his head yet again. *Shit.*

I must have gotten the wrong impression. I thought perhaps he was helping me. He must be doing all of this for some other reason. I glance down at my plate. Why did he feed me? Is he feeding me just to fatten me up or something? Gah. I don't even know what I just ate.

I'm such a naïve fool.

I wiggle my fingers. I try to slip them out of his grasp.

"If we're not friends, I should probably get going then."

His grip tightens and he leans closer. "Mine," he growls.

I about fall over from shock. *Did I just hear that? Did he just speak another word?* There's no way. No freakin' way. I must have heard it wrong.

I yank back hard now, I really want my hand back. "What was that?" I ask.

"Mine," he repeats gruffly. There's no mistaking it now.

I have to be dreaming.

"You're hurting me," I hiss out as his hand crushes my hand.

He let's go and I yank my hand back. If I was dreaming, the pain would have awoken me.

My hand is throbbing. I'm still awake. This isn't a dream.

He stands from the other side of the table. I immediately jump to my feet and start to back away from him.

"Hey, I don't want any problems here..." I say cautiously.

He comes around the side of the table for me. I scoot around the other side keeping the table between us.

"Mine," he growls again.

"No, I don't think so, bub!"

He starts to come for me. I move, keeping the table between us.

"Let's get this straight right now. I'm not yours! And you need to keep your distance!"

He frowns darkly at me then he says softly, "Mine." He forms a fist with his right hand and pounds it against his chest.

I shake my head. I'm not entirely sure what to make of him pounding against his chest, but it's quite obvious he's very serious about what he's saying.

I need him, I know I need him, but I'm not willing to deceive or take advantage of him by leading him on for it. It's best he knows now, I will only be his friend. I can't and won't be more than that. If he can't accept that, or expects more of me, then I'll just have to make another run for it.

"No," I say as harshly as I can and glare at him. I go one step further and place both hands on my hips. I'm making a stand.

He suddenly leaps on top of the table and I squeal, almost falling backward. He reaches for me, trying to grab me. I scramble away just in time. I turn and make a run for it, but it's not a straight shot for the door. I have to swerve between the tables. Unfortunately, he ends up chasing me right into another corner. He's too damn good at it.

"Please," I beg him, holding out my hands in self-defense.

His eyes are glowing again like they're about to explode. He ignores my hands, walking into them, pushing them back as he pushes against me. He's so damn big, this close I have to tip my head back to look up at him.

I'm afraid I've made him mad. My heart is pounding in my chest. I can't catch my breath.

"Please don't hurt me."

I probably shouldn't have said that. I can still feel a faint throb in my hand and now, somehow, he looks even more pissed. He growls. It's such an animalistic sound, something that you would expect from a beast.

And isn't that what he is? He's a Beast.

I tense as his head dips down. I'm expecting a lash of pain, not for him to kiss me.

Our mouths collide and it feels like every nerve in my body is brought screaming to life with electricity. The little jolts I experienced when he kissed my knuckles have nothing on this. The feel of his lips against my lips is all consuming. It's completely overwhelming. I have to reach out and grab onto him before I fall to my knees.

Holding on to his shirt, I can feel something in his chest rumbling as if he's purring. He just holds me there, lips pressing firmly into mine as if that's all he wants to do to me.

I revel in it, I can't help it. Sparks flash behind my eyes. When did I close them? Warm currents of energy are flowing through my body, gathering in the junction between my legs. I don't know why it's happening. I have no explanation for it. I've been kissed before, but it never felt like this. *Nothing has ever felt this amazing.*

He pulls away suddenly leaving me shaking and gasping.

It stops. Everything that happened while he kissed me just fades away. I gape at him in shock. I don't know what to say.

A smug smile forms on his lips. "Mine," he rumbles.

For that briefest of moments, I actually felt as if I was *his*.

***

"You're a Beast!" I hiss at him. "Unhand me!"

I'm shaken up. I literally cannot stop trembling. And I'm so angry but I don't know if I'm angry because he kissed me or because he *stopped* kissing me. It felt as if all that buildup of energy was leading to something...

His head dips forward, smug smile still in place. I stiffen, afraid he's going to kiss me again.

I swear he chuckles as he stops and brushes his lips across my forehead instead. His lips leave behind a trail of hot, sizzling energy.

"Argh! Don't do that!" I cry out and shove at his chest. It's not that it doesn't feel good, what he's doing, it's that he's doing it without asking. I've got to draw the line somewhere or this is going to get out of hand, fast.

He takes a step back and holds his hand out to me.

"You want me to go somewhere with you?" I ask, incredulous, as I look at his hand. "After what you just did to me?"

He nods his head at me and his hand remains.

"I'm not going to bed with you if that's where you're wanting to take me…"

His eyes flash. I feel hot just looking at them. I probably shouldn't have given him that idea. If he really wanted to take me to his bed, all he would have to do is throw me over his shoulder again and carry me. Then, to keep me from fighting too much, all he would have to do is kiss me…

What is wrong with me?

Beast shakes his head, but his eyes are still roaming over me. So hot. So red. I'm burning.

I shiver and wrap my arms around myself, "Lead the way."

He stares at me.

I sigh. I know what he wants and I don't like it. I don't want to touch him again or for him to touch me. But I like it less standing here while he stares at me. I don't like what's it's doing to me. I don't like the way I'm thinking…

"Fine," I say begrudgingly and place my hand, the one that is still throbbing, in his hand. I feel the jolt again when our skin connects, but I swear this time it's stronger and the sharp jolt heads straight for my belly.

It's not until after he's led me down the halls and around all the corners that I realize that my hand is no longer throbbing. I don't feel even a hint of pain.

He hesitates before a door, shifting from foot to foot as if he's uneasy about something. I have to wonder what could make him uneasy.

Finally, he grumbles something low, as if he doesn't want me to hear it. *Ah, he doesn't want me to learn the voice commands.*

The door opens, dropping out of view. I'm so turned around by what's happened, by all the weird feelings and emotions, I didn't even realize he was leading me back to the room I slept in last night.

By the hand, Beast leads me forward, then just as I'm in the room, he releases my hand and walks back out.

"You're leaving me?" I ask.

He nods his head and grumbles.

The door rises from the floor. I feel myself pouting.

For some reason, right now, I don't like the thought of being separated from him. Watching him disappear from my sight fills me with a strange intense yearning feeling.

I hear him stomping down the hall. With each step he takes, the yearning increases.

What did he do to me? Did he feed me some weird alien aphrodisiac?

After a couple of minutes, I hear the faint sounds of air pressure releasing. He's exiting the ship. There's a slight rattle then the sounds of air pressure again.

As time passes, the yearning feeling eases. I can't help but wonder where he is going and what he is doing. Minutes tick by, he doesn't come back.

I feel like I can breathe. I flex my fingers. My hand no longer hurts. Did it heal? Maybe I overreacted and he didn't really hurt me.

With nothing else in the room and nothing else to do, I decide to try the bed out. I stretch myself out on it. It's so soft. So comfortable. I had forgotten what a bed felt like.

I close my eyes and start to drift off to sleep. I see his face. His eyes are burning into me, searing me. I flush with heat. I can't sleep. I'm on the most comfortable thing I've felt in days, maybe weeks, and I can't stop tossing and turning.

I can't get comfortable because I can't stop thinking of him. I can't stop wondering *Why did he leave me?*

CHAPTER THIRTEEN

The sound of Beast purring awakens me. My eyes fly open and he's there, beside me, on the bed. He's propped himself up on one arm and he's looming over me.

"You're back," I say softly.

He stares at me and nods his head.

I don't know what to say, all the questions I want to ask require more than yes or no answers. *Where did you go? What did you do? How long were you gone? Why are you next to me, looking at me like that?*

He bends forward and I fear he's going in for the kiss. If he kisses me here, on the bed, I don't know if I'll be able to handle it. I fear I won't be able to resist giving in to him. I roll myself away and end up rolling myself off the bed.

"Ugh," I grumble as I push myself off the floor and get to my feet.

He reacts fast. I feel him towering above me, invading my personal space.

"Hey, I'm okay."

His hands touch my shoulders and I jerk away.

"Don't touch me."

He frowns at me and pulls back. I shake my head at him. No more touching. I don't even want him near me until I can figure out why I'm reacting to him like I am.

"Did you drug me?" I ask and cross my arms over my chest.

Beast grumbles, his eyes narrowing and shakes his head.

"Did you put something in the meat?"

He snorts and I narrow my eyes back at him.

"I'm just trying to figure out what's going on here."

His eyes fill with understanding. He thumps his fist against his chest and says, "Mine."

"Stop saying that!"

A look of hurt appears on his face. Dammit, I don't want to upset him but I don't know how else to handle this. I can't just go along with this whole "Mine" thing.

"I'm sorry," I apologize. "It's just...." I want to say *ridiculous* but instead I say, "I need some space. Please."

He takes a step back. It's a start.

"Thank you."

He nods his head and takes another step back from me.

He's giving me what I need, but I don't feel even the least bit happy. In fact, for some strange reason, I'm a little upset he's moving away.

It's like my mind and body aren't on the same page. If they don't sync soon, it's going to drive me crazy. *Maybe I already have a touch of the space madness.*

After a couple of tense, silent minutes, I begin to feel like I need to relieve myself. I don't know how long it's been since I last used the portable potty, but now it's catching up to me.

I shift my weight from foot to foot and ask, "Do you happen to have a bathroom here?"

Beast nods and eagerly holds out his hand.

I shake my head at him. I still don't want him to touch me. "Just show me the way."

He shakes his head and grabs my hand anyway. It feels as if I was just struck by lightning. The breath and all my thoughts go flying out of me.

Before I can protest, he pulls me out the door and down the hallway. I don't even feel my feet touching the floor before he stops in front of a door that is actually marked with some paint. He grumbles something and the door slides down, but I try to commit the painted symbol to memory.

A gush of warm, moist air washes over me. It's not just a toilet, I realize as we step inside and the door closes behind me, it's a fully functional bathing facility.

"You have showers!" I gasp.

There's not just a row of open showers lining the wall in the back, there's also a giant pool of water in the middle of the room, steaming and bubbling.

He lets go of my hand and for a moment I forget I really need to pee. I rush forward in my excitement, right up to the edge of the bathing pool and dip my toes in. It's so warm, so inviting. I shiver and my skin prickles with goosebumps.

I feel him coming up behind me. I pull my foot out and turn, afraid I'll need to keep him from touching me. Instead, I find him stripping off his shirt. Then, while I'm gaping at the sight of his broad muscled chest, he removes his pants.

He grins. I instantly flush with heat.

"What are you doing?" I stammer and advert my eyes.

It's too late, though, I've already gotten a good look and the sight of him will forever be branded into my memory. He's just as big as I remember him. Too massive and imposing. The size of him is not only awe inspiring and breathtaking, it's also a very good reminder I need to be very, very careful about what I'm doing.

It's very obvious he wants to… mate with me. Even if I did start to give in and find myself wanting his affections, there's no way we could physically work. I may have zero personal experience when it comes to sexual relations, but I'm not idiot, I know there's no chance, no physical way that what he's packing between his legs will fit inside my body.

He'd break me.

I scan the room, searching for the toilet, searching for my out. Just as Beast starts walking towards me, I spot it. In the very back there's a door with a big green button. I skirt around the pool and break for it.

I run up to the door, jam the green button and the door drops. I jump in the stall, turn around, and catch a glimpse of him as he steps down into the bubbling water. I punch the button and the door slides up again. I take way more time than I need to.

***

Beast's people and my people must have a lot in common, despite our physical differences. We have space ships and wear clothes. We sleep in rooms with beds and use similar bathing facilities. We like to eat the same things. I just wish I could understand what he speaks.

I wonder if his species is a member of the Transgalatic Alliance? If they are, then he's obligated to aid me.

While I kill time in the potty, I try to think of all the different species I was forced to memorize during my political science studies.

I'm sitting on the toilet, my face scrunched up in deep thought when he bangs on the door.

Startled, I scream.

The door starts vibrating and screeching. *Is he trying to rip it out?*

"Stop! Please!" I wail, completely freaked out.

The screeching stops, but I hear him grumble
something completely unintelligible.

I can hear my heart thundering in my ears. I
quickly stand and push the red button on the wall.
The red switches to green and the door vibrates
with an ominous rattle. He hits the door again, I
shriek. The door gives one last groan before finding
its track and dropping down the slit in the floor,
disappearing.

"Are you trying to give me a heart attack?!"
pops out of my mouth as soon as I see him.

It takes me a moment to realize that not only is
he standing there, dripping wet, with his shoulders
bulging forward, as if he's about to break
something, but he's also still utterly naked.

My eyes drop down, I can't help it. I stare as if
hypnotized at what he's packing. He seems to like
my attention. His shoulders straighten, his feet
spread, and his manhood rises.

"Oh, my stars!" I gasp out and look away. "Do
you not have any towels around here?"

Do you need to borrow some shame?

He speaks something.

I shake my head, keeping my eyes averted. "I'm
not looking until you cover that...yourself up."

He grumbles and then grabs me by the hand.
He pulls me out of the stall and I stumble forward.

"Hey!" I look up, afraid I'm going to fall on my
face. "What's going on? What are you doing?"

Beast doesn't answer me. I wouldn't be able to understand him if he did anyway, unless of course the answers were *Ameia* or *Mine*.

He leads me to the edge of the bathing pool.

I start to ask, "Do you want me to get in?"

He releases my hand. Before I realize what's happening or even have a chance to stop him, he grabs the bottom of my shirt and yanks it up, over my head.

I shriek and grab for the shirt.

"What are you doing! Give me that back!"

I feel like we're children and he's playing a game of keep-away as he holds the shirt up, out of my reach.

"Please," I plead with tears stinging my eyes.

He frowns at me and shakes his head.

I have half a mind to knee him to get the shirt back. I think he realizes it because he turns slightly away from me. He tosses my shirt away.

"No!" I moan.

He grabs me by the hand and his fingers tighten as if he knows I'm going to fight him. He steps down into the bubbling pool of water and pulls me in with him.

Hidden beneath the bubbling surface of the water are a set of steps. When my feet touch down on the first step, I yank back in protest.

"Let go of me. I can bathe myself."

Beast sharply shakes his head and pulls me down to the next step.

The last thing I want to do is make him angry. I need his help. I need his protection. I need him to trust me enough so I can explore this ship. But I so don't want to get in this bath with him. Nothing good can come of this. Nothing good can come of us being so close together, both of us naked.

So far, he's backed off when I let him know he was going too far but I'm afraid something has changed. Now he seems to be completely ignoring my protests. I don't know if he'll stop now. I don't think I'll be able to stop him.

I shiver as the warmth of the bath seeps into my flesh. First the water reaches my knees, then my hips, and finally, when my feet touch the bottom, it comes up to my breasts.

I wish the bath was deeper. I wish it would cover me and hide me from him. *I wish it would cover more of him.*

He leads me to the center of the pool then turns to face me. By the hand, he keeps me trapped.

I should be enjoying this, my first hot bath in ages. If I was alone, I'd scrub off all the stickiness then cozy up to the ledge and soak for hours. I'd let the water and the steam cleanse all the impurities from my pores until I felt like a princess again.

There's not enough space between us, only inches. I try to sink down into the water. With his other hand, he grabs me by the shoulder and pulls me back up.

"Why?" I ask.

Beast shakes his head and lets go of my shoulder.

I look up at his face to meet his eyes, but he's looking at my hair. "I'm not comfortable with this."

He grabs one of my blonde curls then twists it around his purple finger. He seems fascinated by it.

"I want you to stop touching me."

He shakes his head.

"I don't like you touching me."

I don't like it because each touch, no matter how faint, is sizzling and electric. My hand is tingling and my shoulder still feels warm.

That gets his attention. His red eyes flick up to meet mine and he arches his brow.

The way he regards me, it reminds me too much of my stepbrother Vrillum. Vrillum has a way of arching his brow and smirking that always makes me feel like I'm beneath him. And I'm the princess, he's not even a prince.

"I mean it."

Beast drops my curl and smirks. He turns away, then pulls me with him as he walks to the other end of the pool.

I'd dig in my heels if the bottom of the pool wasn't so slick. He leads me to a ledge where baskets of bottles and stacks of towels have been placed. He grabs up a clear bottle and sniffs at it.

Turning back to me, he holds out the bottle.

I have to ask, "You want me to smell it?"

He nods his head.

I so don't understand any of this. He completely ignores my protests when I make it clear that I don't want to take a bath with him. Ignores me when I tell him I don't want him to touch me. Yet, he wants me to smell the bottle? How does that make any sense?

"Why do you care what I think? You've ignored what I've wanted so far."

He shrugs and turns away. He puts that bottle back then grabs up another one. He goes through all the bottles, sniffing them one by one until he finally settles on one he likes. Grasping a white bottle, he turns back to me.

He releases my hand and squirts some soap from the bottle into his giant palm. I start to back away from him, though, I know I won't be able to escape. He tosses the bottle away, quickly grabs me, and pulls me back.

"What are you doing?" I ask as he lightly slaps his palm on top of my head.

He wipes his palm off with my hair, then digs his fingers in and begins to massage my scalp.

"Oh, my stars," I gasp.

It feels amazing. My eyes almost roll back in my head. His strong fingers knead at my scalp, digging and working. I don't know how I'm still standing on my feet. Tendrils of pleasure flow through me, his ministrations leave me feeling weak in the knees.

He just literally turned me to putty in his hands.

Suds start to drip down from my forehead, threatening to spill into my eyes. His fingers carefully brush the tiny bubbles away, but I still close my eyes. Suddenly I'm spinning. I want to look, want to see what's happening, but the promising sting of the soap keeps me from chancing it.

His fingers drag down my cheek then he's nudging my chin up. I tip back my head, obeying him. I should protest, a part of me knows I should put up some kind of fight. To give in so easily will just encourage him to continue to believe he can take liberties with me. *It just feels so damn good.*

He rinses my hair out. Cupfuls of warm water flow over me, down my shoulders, down my back. His fingers comb through my hair, working out the kinks and knots.

He's taking care of me. The way he's handling me with his slow, tender movements I feel special, maybe even appreciated.

I peek my eye open and I see him gazing down affectionately at me. *How can someone so scary be so soft? What have I done to deserve this?*

"Mine," he growls softly.

I shiver and wish he hadn't said that. He totally just ruined the moment.

So far he hasn't touched my body, only my hair and face. His hands come down on my shoulders and I instantly tense.

This is it, I think. The air is fairly sizzling now with electricity. He's naked, dripping wet naked. His purple skin gleams, slick and glistening. He's so…massive. I'm naked, and now I'm clean. Did he wash me to have his way with me?

Beast's fingers squeeze my shoulders tenderly and he steps away from.

Seriously?

He waves his hand at the bottles, as if encouraging me to use them, then turns from me and steps out of the pool. I watch him, watch the muscles in his cheeks flex as he rises from the water. He circles around the edge of the pool, walking stiffly and as far away from me as he can. My eyes follow him every step of the way. I'm frozen with disbelief.

Beast walks to the row of shower stalls in the back, opens a door, and disappears.

That's it? He washes my hair and then takes off? I still can't believe it. I don't know what to make of this and I don't know how long I have before he returns.

My first thought is to get out of the pool and sneak off to do some exploring. But it's doubtful I'll have enough time to accomplish anything worth accomplishing. For all I know he's gone to fetch something and is coming right back. No, it's better that for now, I do what he asks. I need to build trust with him, so when the time is right, I can take advantage of it.

This is a good sign. This is a sign that he's building some trust with me. But why do I feel like I was just rejected?

I drift over to the assortment of bottles and pick through them. I choose a scent that reminds me of the roses back home and begin to wash myself. I keep an eye out for Beast, expecting him to return at any moment. I keep fearing he'll catch me washing my more private areas, such as my breasts or between my legs, but thankfully, he never shows.

I grow tired of standing while waiting for him to come back. I wade over to the steps, take a seat on the lowest one and lean back. My legs stretch out before me, and I close my eyes as I try to relax.

Just minutes ago, I couldn't have felt more relaxed. The way he touched me, massaged me, and took care of me, I never felt more cherished. And that's exactly it, isn't it? It felt like he cared for me, like I was important to him.

But why? Why did he do it? He forced me into the bath, knowing I wasn't comfortable with it, knowing that I didn't want it, just to wash my hair? How absurd is that? He could have done anything to me. He's stronger than me, can easily overpower me, he'd have little trouble forcing himself on me…. *Don't go there, Ameia.*

I completely dropped my guard as soon as his fingers touched my head. I gave in. Whatever fears or trepidations I have, he kneaded right out of me. *When he touches me, it's like I become a different person.* A person without a brain, clearly.

The tile beneath my head begins to vibrate. I open my eyes to see him approaching me. He's dressed in boots, black pants, and black shirt. In his arms, he's holding a big, fluffy white thing. I can't think of a way to get out of the water without flashing him all my naked bits.

He walks right up to me and snaps out the white fluffy thing. It's a white robe and he's holding it out for me to slip myself in. One arm crosses over my breasts as I sit up and then get to my feet. He steps up to me and drapes the robe over my shoulders. While I wiggle my arms into the sleeves, he let's go, then from behind, he wraps the robe snuggly around me and ties the belt at my hip.

There he goes again, taking care of me. Going above and beyond to give me more than I need, pampering me. *Like a bossy servant.* Perhaps he's only doing it to try and win my affections? Just as I'm attempting to build trust with him...

"Thank you," I say sincerely, even though I'm wary of his motives.

He nods his head and without asking, takes me by the hand. It's then that I notice that instead of being warmed by his touch, like before, I'm chilled by his clammy palm and fingers.

"Oh, you're cold," I shiver.

He frowns and drops my hand.

Did he take a cold shower or something?

Either way, I enjoy following him as he leads me to the mess hall without being forced to hold his hand.

CHAPTER FOURTEEN

After preparing and feeding me another tasty meal of mystery meat and strange fruit, my purple alien captor leads me back to my room and locks me in. I stretch out on the bed, still engulfed in my soft, fluffy robe. There's too much softness, too much fluffiness. I'm clean, fed, and relaxed. I sleep deeply and dream.

It's my 18th birthday party. It feels as if half the planet is squeezed inside the palace ballroom. It's truly a crush in every sense of the word.

I need to get away from the watchful eyes and whispered rumors. I can't handle crowds or large groups of strangers. I can't handle all the attention. There are too many people and not enough air or space. I'm suffocating in the press of bodies.

All night the focus has been centered on me. The weight of their judgment is smothering me. I'm cracking. I'm not worthy in their eyes. Everywhere I look, someone is pointing at me. Everywhere, someone is laughing.

My heart is racing, I'm cold and sweaty. I feel like I can't breathe. I don't know where my guards are, they've disappeared. I lost them somewhere in the crush, and now there's no one to help me.

Someone grabs me by the arm and drags me through the crowd. For some reason I can't see them, they're simply a force propelling me forward. The crowd parts for us even as they continue laughing at me. It's not until my captor hauls me up on the podium in the center of the ballroom that I realize it's my father, the King.

The King stands beside me, dressed in his finest finery. He wears his long purple cape over his golden silk suit. His silver beard has been brushed and braided in a weave over his chin. A gold and diamond encrusted crown engraved with the shapes of stars encircling our planet is poised perfectly on his bald head.

The crowd falls silent, waiting for the King to speak. My father's voice booms but his words don't make any sense. I can't understand what he's saying. He keeps speaking and the crowd seems to be following. Then in horror, it dawns on me. He's speaking in grunts and growls. He's speaking like Beast.

As if I summoned him just by thinking of him, Beast appears. He's wet, naked, and heading straight for me. He climbs the podium and takes my hand. I look down and see I'm also wet and naked as he takes his place beside me.

The crowd erupts in cheers. People start hugging each other and lifting their glasses as if they're toasting us. My father turns to me and smiles. On his face, all I can see is his natural love and affection for me.

"Mine," Beast growls and lifts my hand in the air as if we're sharing a victory.

The crowd goes wild, then they all start to roar, "Your's! Your's! Your's!"

I look to the crowd and then back to my father for help, but now my father is also chanting. "Your's! Your's! Your's!"

I wake up vowing to never again fall asleep.

***

I'm going stir crazy in the room. After tossing and turning on the bed, I couldn't go back to sleep. I didn't want to go back to sleep.

Hours have crept by. I've explored every inch of this room and have found absolutely nothing of interest. I've run my fingers along the walls, checked under the mattress, and even scrutinized the ceiling. If there's anything to be found, I'm not going to find it.

The panel of buttons on the wall leaves me even more frustrated. After pushing every single button, in as many combinations that I could think of, nothing happens. I know, that at the very least, it should be able to open the closet. He must have disabled it, or it has some crazy long sequence I'll never be able to guess.

Out of options, I try my hand at the voice commands. I can remember the general rhythm of the words he spoke and do my best to recreate it. I grumble and growl until my throat is raw before giving up. Even to my own ears, I know I'm missing all the nuances.

The only way I'm getting out of this room is if he lets me out.

I pace in front of the door, wondering where Beast is. Time drags on. *When is he going to return? I need to get out. What does he do when he's not with me? Is he out hunting? Or is he up to something else?*

I hope and pray he's not up to anything dangerous. If anything happens to him, I'll be stuck in here. I'll die in here. Alone.

It feels like it takes forever before he finally comes for me, though it's probably only been an hour or so since I woke up. I spend the time not only trapped in the room but trapped inside my thoughts.

How long have I've been in this ship? How many days have passed? If someone from home does show up, I'll never know.

When the door drops, I can't believe I'm actually happy to see him. I was beginning to make myself sick with worry. And I had an unexplainable achy feeling in the pit of my stomach that disappears as soon as my eyes touch him.

He walks in carrying a stack of clothing topped with a pair of boots.

"Are those for me?" I ask.

He nods, walks up to me, and thrusts out the stack. Gratefully, I accept them. He takes a step back, staring at me. I look down at the clothing, then back up to him.

After a minute passes, I ask, "Do you want me to get dressed?"

Beast nods.

I frown, "I need some privacy…"

I don't care how many times he's already seen me naked. I'm so not going willingly expose myself in front of him.

He sighs and grumbles as he walks out the door. I shake off the robe and leave it on the bed, for later. I pull the black shirt over my head then stuff myself inside the tight black pants. Just as I suspected, he walks back in only a second later. I button the pants then sit on the edge of the bed to put the socks and boots on.

Everything fits snugly. It's not too tight, comfort wise, but modesty-wise, without undergarments, I'm out of luck. I suppose I could ask him for a brassiere but… how do I even ask that? Does he even know what one is? What if he's used to the females from his planet being naked all the time? I don't even want to go there, especially after our last encounter. He forced himself on me, to wash my hair. Things with him can get very weird, very quick.

"Are we going somewhere?" I ask, hopeful.

I stand from the bed, smooth my hands down my new outfit and smile. It feels good to be completely covered for once. I feel dressed to take on the world.

He nods his head and the corners of his lips curve into a smile. So far, we're off to a good start. Until he holds out his hand.

I frown at his hand. I don't want to touch him. *Why can't he just let me follow him?*

My hesitation turns his smile into a frown.

Dammit, the last thing I want to do right now is make him mad. What if he changes his mind and decides to leave me here?

At that thought, I practically jump forward and slap my hand against his.

"Shall we?" I close my fingers around him and try to ignore the zap that travels up my arm.

If I knew where we were going, I'd pull him out of the room and drag him down the hall myself. As it is, I have to wait for him to lead the way.

His frown deepens and his brow knits. I'm sure my sudden change of heart confuses him. Then he shrugs and leads me out of the room.

My heart races with excitement as we pass the bathing facilities, turn around the corner, then pass the mess hall. I'm so eager to get out of this ship, to have sky above me and fresh air all around me, I'm able to keep pace with him. His long, brisk stride gives me no trouble at all.

We make a stop at a supply room where he lets go of my hand and outfits me with a water bladder that I wear like a backpack on my back. He outfits himself in what I'm assuming is a utility belt. Then, with a voice command, he opens up a locked locker.

He has guns! He has weapons! He produces two small guns from the locker, inspects them, and then straps them securely to his belt. Before I can get a better, closer look at all the stuff he has stored in the locker, he slams it shut and walks up to a shelf loaded with ammo. While he loads himself up, I take a better look around.

The entire supply room is bursting with goodies I'm itching to get my hands on. Everything one would need to survive in an unforgiving harsh environment seems to be right here. There are knives displayed on the wall and shelves covered in tools, emergency medical kits, portable lights, and ration bars. There are giant jugs of crystal clear water stacked and piled up in the corners.

Why haven't I see him with any of this stuff before?

I'm eyeing the knives on the wall, there's one with a wicked curve to its blade and sharp serrated teeth. It's calling me, it's practically crooning my name. I begin to reach for the knife. I rise up on my tiptoes, the tips of my fingers brush across the hilt.

I freeze when I hear Beast growl behind me.

His hands come down on my shoulders and I lower back down.

"What, don't you trust me?" I ask as I tip my head back and peer up at him through my lashes.

It was more of a joke, really. If I were him, I sure as hell wouldn't trust me. He's keeping me here, with him, totally against my will. He has all the power, all the control. Stick a weapon in my hands and all that could change in a flash.

He seems to be conflicted by my question, though. His eyes narrow thoughtfully, then he reaches over my shoulder and plucks the knife from the wall.

I freeze as he pulls the knife back. He lifts the knife over my head and turns the blade as he admires its different gleaming angles. His thumb pricks the tip, then he takes the blade between his fingers and flips the hilt towards me.

He's just testing me…

I meet his eyes over the blade. His brows quirk as if to ask me what am I waiting for…

"I can take it?" I ask.

I'm not touching the knife unless I know I have his permission. After all, I wouldn't want him to get the wrong impression in this situation and end me right here, right now.

He nods.

Still, my hand is trembling as I reach out and grab the hilt. I just can't believe he's actually giving me a weapon. It still feels like a test, like this whole thing is some trick question, and I'm about to fail.

My fingers wrap around the hilt and he let's go. He takes a step back and I spin to face him, knife securely in hand.

This is it. He's standing right there, completely vulnerable. *Now, I have the means to end him.* If I lunge forward, I can bury this knife deep in his chest. He may be alien, but I know for a fact that just like me, he's made up of flesh and bone.

I know he knows what I'm thinking. Our eyes meet and yet he still just stands there, leaving himself completely open, waiting for me to make a move.

I know if I kill him now, this ship is mine. I probably won't be able to get back inside the room I was sleeping in, or back inside the bathing facilities, but I'll have all of the supplies in this storage room to myself. I could hold out for a year or more on this stuff. I could use something to break down the front door. All I would have to do is find a means to keep an eye out for rescue.

But does he deserve to die? Do I even have the guts to do it?

What has he done to me but terrify me? He's protected me, clothed me, and fed me... all against my will.

I take a deep, shuddering breath. The moment is passing. I failed to take advantage of it. I point the knife down. I'm not necessarily a violent person. Just thinking about killing him has left me feeling sick to the stomach. Until he does something that actually harms me, I won't try to harm him. There are other ways, nonviolent ways, to take back my freedom. I'll just have to figure it out.

Beast huffs, the sound pulls me out of my thoughts. The knife feels awkward in my hand now. I fidget with it, not sure what to do with it. He turns his back on me. *If that isn't a sign of trust, I don't know what is.* He moves to a shelf, grabs up a belt and then tosses it to me. I catch the belt with my free hand.

I tell him, "Thank you," set my knife down, and secure the belt around my waist. After picking the knife back up, I sheathe it at my right hip.

He walks up to the door, I half expect him to keep on walking. He stops, however, and turns back around. He holds out his hand.

Did I pass the test? I wonder as I tentatively approach him and lay my hand on his. I feel guilty for even considering killing him. I mean, he's done so much for me. I'm sure if we could actually communicate with words, he'd have a perfectly good reason for all this....

Who am I kidding? It's just a matter of time before the guy eats me.

His fingers curl around me, I look up. A smile is beginning to form on his lips.

"So, where are we going?" I ask.

He lifts my hand to his face and then kisses it. As soon as his lips make contact with my skin, I feel like someone just punched me in the gut. All the air whooshes out of me. I sway on my feet. Not again. I groan inwardly as electric sensations flow through me and pulse between my thighs. Somehow, I think he's doing this on purpose. *Why does it only happen some of the time and not others?*

He touches my hand to his chest, over his heart.

"Mine," he purrs.

His chest is vibrating so hard, the bones in my hand feel like they're rattling.

On second thought, maybe I should have stabbed him...

My eyes narrow murderously. He tips his head back and laughs before leading me out the door.

CHAPTER FIFTEEN

I squint against the bright sunlight as we step outside. The air releases hiss, I sense the doors closing behind us. How many days has it been since I last seen the sun? I'd ask, but it's not a yes or no kind of answer.

The last time I was here, I was thrown over his shoulder and couldn't see where we were going. Curiously, I look around. His ship is in the middle of a field, out in the open.

I spin around to look at his ship. Funny, it doesn't look like it crashed. There are no grooves in the dirt, no visible outside damage to the hull. Given the massive size of the ship, it would have made quite the dent if it touched down or at least left a grassy skid mark. It looks like it landed here, intentionally.

Beast waits patiently for me to have my look and then tugs on my hand. I sigh and turn back to him. My fingers itching to escape his grasp.

"So, which way are we going?" I ask.

He points straight ahead and leads me across the grassy blue-green field.

Maybe it's because I'm out in the sun, inhaling fresh air, but I feel like I'm in a pretty good mood. Like I could start skipping right now, across this field. It's good to have something to do, to have a purpose, even though I don't know what the purpose is. I've spent so long, just sitting around, waiting for something to happen, it feels awesome to make something happen.

And, because of this good mood, I feel like talking. I know all I'm going to get out of tall, dark, and purple is grunts and growls, but that's okay. I can talk enough for the both of us.

"Is your home planet far from here?"

He nods.

"Is that your ship back there?"

He shakes his head.

Oh, that's interesting. Too bad I can't just ask whose ship it is.

"Did you steal that ship?

He nods his head.

"Seriously?"

He smirks at me.

"Is the owner going to come looking for it?"

He looks like he has to think for a moment before shaking his head.

"You didn't kill them... did you?"

He starts to nod and I gasp. He smirks at my reaction and then shakes his head.

Is he teasing me?

I narrow my eyes at him.

"Did you or didn't you?"

He lifts both of his dark brows then wiggles them playfully. He'd look silly if his eyes weren't red and glowing.

"Ugh. What's that supposed to mean?"

He chuckles and then says something in his weird alien language.

I can't understand it so I just roll my eyes. *If only he spoke Common. Which reminds me…*

"Is your homeworld a member of the Transgalatic Alliance?"

He snorts and sharply shakes his head.

"Wow. There are not many planets or species that I can think of that aren't." I think out loud.

He says something else and motions dismissively with his hand. I get the feeling he doesn't think highly of the Alliance.

"Well, my planet has been a member for only a little over a millennia now. We're a bit late to the party."

He snorts.

"I know many of the other planets look at us like we're backwards like we haven't finished evolving yet. Especially since our women are the rulers."

He brings us to a stop and for a moment, I think he's actually interested in what I'm saying. Then he touches his mouth and shakes his head. I take it that he wants me to be quiet.

I sigh and nod.

I can see trees off in the distance. The sun is high in the sky. We have hours before dark. We set off again. The ground is flat and just grassy. It's easy going until we get to the trees.

The change in atmosphere is striking. Out in the field, it's warm, bright, and sunny. In the trees, it's dark and cool with the sun blocked out by the thick cover of leaves.

I shiver and wonder just what exactly are we doing out here. I was hoping he'd lead me back to my pod, or I'd at least get a glimpse of it, to check on it.

He starts to lead me into the trees and I pull back my hand. I don't want to go into the forest. The forest is full of small, fuzzy little creatures who want to eat me.

Beast looks at me, his eyes questioning.

"Why do you want to go in there?"

Now is one of those times where it would really come in handy to be able to verbally communicate with him. He grumbles something I can't understand.

"I'll stay here," I say softly.

He shakes his head and pulls on my hand.

I stubbornly dig in my heels and pull back.

He grumbles and glares at me.

"I am not going in there," I glare back.

He pulls on my arm, making me take a step forward.

"No," I hiss. "There are evil fuzzballs in there who want to kill me."

Our eyes meet, locked in a silent battle of wills. If his eyes didn't glow, I would so win this staring contest. I start to see spots, though. I have to look away. It was like staring into a light for too long. Or two burning red suns.

"You're such a cheater," I pout in defeat.

He tugs impatiently on my hand. He won fair and square. I bow my head as I follow him in. I just have such a bad feeling about this.

I'm so on edge, each snapping twig has me practically jumping out of my skin. I keep expecting to hear a chirp or see a pair of beady black eyes watching me from the trees. All I want to do is turn tail and run back to the safety of the ship.

Deeper and deeper we walk into the forest. It's eerily silent and gives me the creeps.

Is there nothing else around but us? Or is everything frightened off because my companion is the biggest, baddest, thing here?

I look at Beast, remembering how I myself cowered in my pod, afraid of him. For days.

A misty fog begins to form around us, making it harder and harder for me to see. I'm going on blind faith as I put down one foot in front of the other. By miracle alone, I don't trip over anything. It helps that Beast walks in front of me, still holding my hand, kicking everything out of the way.

It feels like we've been walking for hours, in silence no less, when the fog begins to clear and I can hear the soft, trickling sounds of water somewhere in the distance. The sounds of water grows louder and louder, and then I see it. The very first pool of water I discovered.

Which means my pod isn't far from here.

I half expect Beast to lead me over to the pool of water, but he leads me instead to a cluster of trees half a span away.

Someone made a little hiding place.

The native foliage has been built up around the cluster of trees to provide cover. Beast leads me around until we're behind the trees then motions for me to lower to the ground. The way the leaves and vines are woven around the tree trunks, it provides the perfect camouflage.

A blanket of leaves has already been piled on top of the dirt. Beast lowers down to his knees, settling on the pile, then by the hand, he pulls me down beside him.

I bet he's been here many times before. And I bet he has more than one little hidey spot like this set up around here.

I shudder. *There's probably one near my pod.*

My shudder draws his concern. He squeezes my hand and gives me an inquiring look.

I shake my head at him and whisper, "It's nothing."

He nods and touches his fingers against his lips. At least I know what that means. Well, at least I think it means be quiet. I nod, to say I understand. He finally let's go of my hand. *Hallelujah.*

He leans forward. His large purple hands go to the weapons in his belt while he peers through a small gap in the cover. I have to wonder if his glowing eyes are going to scare whatever he's hunting away. And that's what we're doing, isn't it? We're hunting something. Otherwise, why go through all this trouble to conceal ourselves? Why outfit ourselves with weapons? Now comes the hardest part, I know, from the single hunt I attended with my father, the waiting.

I'm so sick and tired of waiting. The minutes drag by. I shift and squirm restlessly. I lean forward, peek through a gap, but after five minutes of nothing, I lean back. I have no patience.

Time continues to move at a snail's pace. It gets to the point where I'm seriously resenting him for bringing me. I almost wish I was back at the ship. At least I could stretch out, jump on the bed, *do* something. Kneeling on the leaves out here and being quiet is killing me. I want to scream just to break the silence.

Then all of a sudden he tenses. *He must see something.*

I lean forward, look through the gap, and then I see it. It's a squat, fat little creature on four stubby legs. It reminds me of a pig. *Is that what we're hunting?*

It's not that big, I'd say it's about a fourth of the size of a full grown hog. It could be a baby. I glance back to Beast. He has his guns in his hands now. *He can't seriously be considering killing a baby? Oh my stars, is that what he's been feeding me?*

I look back through the gap. My pulse has quickened and I'm filled with unease.

The creature wanders closer and closer to the water. From what I can see, it has its head dropped down, and its nose pushing through the leaves.

Should I try to stop Beast from killing it? I don't know. What if it's the only thing we can eat for meat?

Sure it's small, but that doesn't necessarily make it a baby. The fuzzy creatures I encountered were small too, and seriously evil. They had the cutest eyes but being cute didn't stop them from trying to take a bite out of me.

Still, I have the strongest urge that I need to protect that creature as if it was a baby. Beast shifts beside me. I flick a quick glance at him, but he's still kneeling with his weapons in his hands, but he isn't aiming at it or anything. If he is going to kill it, I don't know why he's waiting.

The creature reaches the water. I can't tell from here, but it's probably drinking. Still, Beast doesn't make a move. I almost start to relax, thinking he must not be as heartless as that. I look at him. *Of course he wouldn't hunt a baby...*

A horrible high pitch squeal breaks the silence. Beast jumps to his feet and fires his weapons. It's all over before I even realize what's happening. Weapons still in hand, Beast just walks out of the cover, leaving me.

I jump to my feet. *What the heck just happened?* Beast is walking towards the water. I look to the spot where I last saw the baby. It's not there. There's just a twitching black blob. I don't even know what that blob is. Beast fires a couple more shots at it. It stops twitching.

Where's the baby? Did it get away?

My eyes search and search. I can't see it anywhere. I guess it ran off. Yet, I can't shake this feeling of unease.

Beast walks up to the blob and shoots it again. To be sure, I guess. Then he holsters one gun. He bends down and grabs hold of the blob. It stretches as he lifts it. For a moment, the blob reminds me of slime, especially the way the part that comes off the ground thins until it's more like a dark string. But then, as he starts to drag it away from the water, I can see it's more like a giant worm or snake.

I follow the line of the blob as it stretches out behind Beast as he keeps walking towards me. The tail of it is still in the water. That's when it dawns on me. *He stopped that thing from getting me the first time I came here. That's why he threw that fruit at me.*

How many times did he save my life? All that time, I thought he wanted to kill me, he was just protecting me. *Even from me…*

Beast lets the part of the black thing he's carrying drop to the ground with a heavy thud. Our eyes meet. There are so many things I want to ask him. If only I could understand the things he says.

He breaks contact by turning away. He walks back to the water and hauls the tail of the thing out. It must be heavy. I can see his muscles straining against his shirt, stretching the soft fabric as he's working. He drops the tail of the thing on the bank, wipes beads of sweat from his forehead with the back of his hand, then starts to walk back to me.

Something squeals. I gasp. Beast stops dead in his tracks.

The part of the creature left on the bank starts moving. Beast grabs his gun and fires at it.

"Stop!" I cry out.

Beast turns sideways to glare at me. I have to remind myself that he's not an evil, space demon. *He's not going to eat me. Maybe.*

I gulp then say, "Don't shoot the baby."

He looks at me like I'm crazy. There's another squeal. Part of the black thing on the ground starts to wiggle.

"Please!" I implore him.

Beast shakes his head.

The baby creature emerges from underneath the black thing. I still can't see its face from here, but its entire little body looks like its trembling. I can hear it snorting. *It needs its mommy.*

"Just let it get away!"

Beast seems to hesitate. He looks at me, then back to the baby creature. His brow furrows as if he's thinking.

The baby stops trembling. It takes a couple of steps forward.

"Go! Run back to your mommy!"

The little creature stops then spins around.

It's the ugliest fucking baby I've ever seen.

Maybe I wanted the creature to live so bad because it survived something that could have killed me. Or maybe I just can't bear to witness something dying unless it's actively trying to kill me. Either way, when I look upon the hideous face of the thing I just saved, I immediately know I've made a big mistake.

It has so many teeth!

There are no lips to its mouth, and even if there were lips, they would probably be shredded to ribbons by its layers upon layers of razor sharp, pointy fangs. It's a thing of nightmares, and now it's headed straight for me.

The creature lowers its head and charges forward.

"Kill it! Kill it!" I scream at Beast.

Beast looks back at me with his brow raised as if he's asking if I'm sure.

Meanwhile, the little creature is getting closer and closer to him. It's either going to attack Beast, or bypass him and come directly for me.

I scream, "Please! Just shoot the damn thing!" and back away.

Beast's lips curl into a smirk. He aims his guns and fires off two rounds at the nightmare baby. It squeals and drops to the ground.

"Thank you," I exhale in relief. For a moment there, I was quite afraid that hideous thing was going to get past Beast and get to me, but he's acting as if it's no big deal, so perhaps I shouldn't have even been worried.

Beast nods his head in acknowledgment. I flash him a grateful smile. His face softens and he walks towards me.

From the ground, the little creature lets out a loud, shrill noise. Beast spins around and unloads a few more rounds into its dying, hideous little body. It falls silent but now Beast is rushing towards me, his face marred with lines of worry.

"What's wrong?" I ask as he grabs my hand. The jolt this time isn't so bad. My fingers only twitch a little when he squeezes them.

Beast shakes his head and touches his hand to his lips. He wants me to be quiet.

I sigh, frustrated, and bit worried that he's worried. Maybe he's not worried, I reassure myself. Maybe I'm just reading too much into his expression. *Perhaps he's just afraid we're going to get back late or something? Dinner could be burning.*

By the arm, he tugs me along. I suddenly notice he's leading me in the direction I think my pod is in.

Just thinking about my pod gets me excited. I'm anxious to check the console, to see if I have any messages. Maybe Beast will know how to use the system. Maybe I can get him to send a distress signal for me.

Beast stops all of a sudden and I crash into his back. Before I can get my bearings, he's tugging me by the arm and rushing me in another direction.

"Hey, no, wait!" I protest and try to yank back.

Beast growls and glares back at me.

"We're going the wrong way. My pod is the other way..."

At least I think it is.

Beast again stops suddenly. This time I catch myself before crashing into his back but only because I was already trying to walk the other way.

"What's going on?" I ask.

I look around, I don't see anything out of the ordinary, just a bunch of trees. Beast seems to be listening for something, though. I don't think he likes what he hears because he turns to me and grabs me.

Before I know what's happening or can do anything to stop it, he lifts me up, tosses me over his shoulder, and takes off running.

"What are you doing?!" I ask shrilly.

He smacks me on the butt.

"You put me down right this instant!" I thump on his back.

He keeps on running and smacks me on the butt again.

The nerve! I can't believe he's doing this! I guess this is what I get for forgetting that he's a barbarian.

I look down and consider his ass. I could so give him a killer wedgie. It got his attention last time, and would serve him right for doing this. But with as fast as he's running, I don't want him to fall over and squash me.

We tear through the forest at break-neck speed. I have to admit, he's running faster than I'd be able to keep up with. The trees blur by, brown mixes with blue and green.

Beast stops so fast, I clutch at his back, afraid I'm going to fall off. His shirt slips from my fingers as he grabs me by the hips and lifts me in the air.

I blink and now I have a wooden ladder in front of me.

It's all happening so fast, I can't keep up with it.

Beast impatiently thrusts me into the ladder. I have no choice but to reach out and grab hold of it. He holds on to me until my feet find the rung below me then he lets go. I look down and he's drawing his guns.

What is going on? I look up. The ladder goes so high, there's no way I can make the climb. I haven't climbed anything since I was little, when I was too dumb to be afraid. And this tree is as tall as a building to me. I'm not just deathly afraid of heights, I'm also deathly afraid of falling.

"I can't." I shake my head and take a step down.

Beast growls menacingly. He holsters his guns and grabs me by the butt, pushing me up.

"No, I can't!" I cry. "I'm afraid."

Beast growls some more. He gives me a hard shove. My arms flail as I go above the rung I was holding on to. I have to grab the higher rung that was above my head.

"Stop! Don't make me!"

Beast makes the most awful sound. It sounds like he just got hurt. I look down. He jumps away from me, pulls out his guns, and starts firing.

Oh, no. Did he just get hurt trying to protect me?

I feel sick to my stomach. My feet scramble to find the rung below me. Somehow, I force my arms to go up. *I can do this.* I grab on to the next highest rung above me. *It's not for me, it's for him.* I pull myself up. *Who knows what nasty creatures are down there.*

I glance down. I've only gone up a couple of feet, but the ground and Beast look so far away. *No, don't look down.*

I look up again. *Just grab it, you can do it. He'd do it for you.*

Over and over, rung by rung, I pull myself up until I finally hear Beast stop firing.

Is he below me or did something bad happen to him?

Before I can muster the courage to look down, something grabs my leg and I scream.

A familiar grumble and growl reassures me. It's Beast.

"Is it all clear now? Can I come down?" I ask, but I only get silence for an answer.

Dammit. I tip my head back and look up. I can see what looks like some kind of floor made out of wood planks, but it's still half a tree up.

I'm pretty sure that's where he wants me to go, but I ask anyway, "Do I have to keep going?"

He gives my leg a squeeze. Double dammit. Pretty sure that means I have to climb the rest of the way up.

If only he could throw me over his shoulder and do the climbing for me....

CHAPTER SIXTEEN

I make it. Somehow I make it. Once I reach the top, I have the strongest urge to kiss the wood floor. I'm so relieved just to have something solid beneath me for the moment, I don't care how far up I am. I don't care that I'm hundreds of feet above the ground in a flimsy little house built into a tree.

Beast climbs up just behind me. He grunts as his feet hit the floor and that's when I remember that he might have gotten hurt because of me.

"What happened down there?" I ask before realizing it was a waste of breath.

The tree house has three walls with half a roof over them, all made of wooden planks. There are two corners that are safe. He limps over to the left corner and takes a seat on the floor. I walk over to him and kneel beside his legs.

"How bad is it?" I ask.

His face is emotionless as he looks back at me. He reaches down and starts to roll up the left leg of his black pants.

I gasp. Something tore into him, just above his ankle. He's bleeding, but I can't tell how badly he's hurt.

"May I look?" I ask.

He nods and I scoot closer. It feels as if his eyes are burning into the top of my head as I bend and take a closer look at his wound. His blood is black. It oozes from his wound and makes it pretty much impossible for me to tell just how big the actual wound is.

I sigh and have to think. I need something to soak the blood up with.

"Did you bring a first aid kit?" I remember there were quite a few of them in the storage room.

I peek up and he shakes his head at me.

"Of course you didn't," I think out loud. "I didn't either. All I brought is this knife and the water on my back..."

I forgot I had anything on me. I slip out of the backpack, then reach down and grab my knife.

Beast grumbles something at me. I look up.

"I have no clue what you're saying."

He narrows his eyes and grumbles again.

"Still no clue."

I grab my shirt, pull it away from my stomach and stab it with the knife.

Beast makes a choking noise. I look over at him and for a purple guy, he's looking awfully green.

"Are you alright?"

I use the knife to cut at my shirt some more, then I lay the knife on the floor and start tearing the bottom off.

Before I finish tearing the swath of my shirt off, Beast leans forward and reaches for my knife.

I snatch it first and frown at him, "Mine."

It's the only weapon on this world I have. I won't let him take it away from me.

Beast grumbles and leans back. I narrow my eyes at him and secure the knife in its spot at my hip. I'm not taking any chances.

I rip the rest of my shirt off, exposing my stomach. I'm mostly decent still, what remains of the shirt still covers my breasts, but it's going to be a long night if it gets chilly. I then rip the fabric I have into strips. Balling up one of the strips, I bend over his leg and soak up the blood with it.

Beast doesn't make a sound. I clear away the blood until I can see the damage. His wound doesn't seem to be terribly bad. I mean, it's obvious he got bit by something with sharp teeth, but it looks like there are only a dozen or so deep puncture wounds. The puncture wounds are oozing, and the bleed is slowing. There doesn't appear to be any tearing or ripping. Still, it must have hurt awfully bad to climb up the tree.

"Is it okay if I bandage your leg?"

I don't wait for an answer, I just start doing it. I press a dry bunch of balled up fabric against his wound, then I wrap the strips of fabric I have around it.

"I'm sorry you got hurt because of me," I say softly.

I tie the bandage in a knot then look up at him.

"I'm glad you're okay, though. I was a little worried down there."

He grumbles something and stares at me intensely.

I sigh, "I wish I could understand you."

He nods his head in agreement.

"Do you mind if I sit beside you?"

He pats his lap and I scowl. *Perhaps that was lost in translation?*

"Beside you, not on you," I say as I start to scoot towards the wall.

I grab the backpack and bring it with me. It takes me forever to get settled but once I do, I feel much better with my back up against the wall. Heights make me feel very dizzy. Feeling dizzy and clumsy only increases the fear that I'm going to slip, trip, or fall over the edge.

I was so focused on him, so focused on his injury, I forgot just where we are. I look up, through the open part of the roof. The sky is getting darker. *The clouds are way too close.* I hope we don't have to stay here long.

"Are we staying the night here?"

Please say no. Please say no.

He nods his head.

Dammit.

"We can't go back to the ship?" I ask.

He shakes his head.

"We can't make it to my pod?"

He shakes his head again.

I'm not going to get any sleep at all.

"Who builds a treehouse with only three walls and half a roof?" I ask and take a sip of the water from my backpack. Just then I realize if I need to relieve myself tonight, I'm up a tree, and out of luck. I push the water away in disgust then wrap my arms around myself.

Beast is a quiet presence beside me. No matter how much I try to relax, I feel overly aware of him. There's static in the space between us. It has all the tiny hairs on my body standing on end, pointing at him.

As the sky grows darker, the red glow from his eyes burns brighter. I try not to look at him. I try to keep my eyes glued to the sky. I can't look at him because every time I do, he just looks so damn hungry. *And I have nothing to feed him, though, I'm pretty sure it's me he wants to eat.*

The stars start to appear. At first, there's only a stray one here and there, twinkling lonely in the sky. But as full night falls, I can't recognize the glittering constellations. It makes it all the more real that I'm far away from home. The stars here are too different. Everything here is too different. Oh, how I miss Terrea.

"No one is coming for me," I say sadly. My heart feels like it's breaking just to admit it. "No one is looking for me. I'm stuck here forever."

Beast reaches out and touches my arm. His touch is warm. I didn't realize I was so cold.

"I'm the Princess. All my life they've been drilling into my head how important I am. If I was so important, they would have come for me by now."

I sense Beast scooting closer to me. I don't try to stop him, but I don't encourage him either.

"Maybe no one cares. Maybe they've abandoned me."

Beast grumbles something softly.

I go quiet and then I feel him nudging my shoulder as if he wants me to elaborate. It hurts. It hurts to think I'll never go home again. It hurts even worse because it's all my fault. If I would have only followed the rule, I wouldn't be here.

"It was my birthday party, the night I crashed here. My stepbrother had special surprise for me...."

I close my eyes as I remember.

"I'm not allowed to leave the planet, so I'd never been up before. The next day, my betrothal was to be announced so..."

Beast cuts me off with a menacing growl.

I let him finish growling then look at him to ask, "Are you done?"

He nods.

"Do you want to hear the rest?"

He nods again so I go on, "So it was pretty much my last chance to ever do it. He convinced me we would be back before anyone would even know we were gone."

I trusted Vrillum. When my father married his mother, Sarcia, I welcomed Vrillum with open arms. In my heart, I made a place for him as my brother because he was always so nice to me, even when his mother was distant and cold. Now, I wonder why he was so friendly. If it was all a farce.

"The ride up actually made me sick. I appreciated the thought but immediately wanted to return home. Trillum got angry with me. He called me an ungrateful, spoiled brat and refused to take me back down. He made me feel bad, made me feel guilty for not appreciating the risk he took for me so I apologized and stop asking him to take me back home. Then, out of nowhere, another ship came, and he freaked out. He said they were slavers and they must have known I was on the ship. He put me in the escape pod and told me he would distract them."

I take in a deep breath. I can feel the tears building behind my eyes. My nose starts to sting with the pressure of holding them back.

"The pod went crazy. Instead of safely transporting me to Terrea, it somehow accelerated and crash landed here."

Beast rubs his hand up and down my arm. It would be comforting if it didn't tingle so much.

I look over at him and regret it. His demon eyes are filled with pity which somehow makes me feel even worse. The first tear drops, cold and unwanted against my cheek. Another follows, then another, until Beast becomes one great big red blur.

"I think he planned all of this. I think Vrillum programmed the pod to purposely crash me here and disabled the UPS so no one can find it. I just don't understand why he left me to die here."

The tears really start coming now. Vrillum left me to die here, alone and suffering, on this god forsaken planet. I'll never speak to my father again. I'll never see his smile or hear his voice. He probably thinks I'm dead or something worse. What if he thinks I ran off?

All this time, I've tried not to think about it too much. I've tried to block it out and just focus on surviving. With everything going on, I let myself get consumed by the moment. Now, all this pent up emotion, all this stuff I've been too afraid to face has me bawling my eyes out. The tears just keep coming and I don't know how to turn them off.

At some point, Beast wraps his arms around me and pulls me into his lap. I fall asleep crying my heart out while snuggled up against the warmth of his chest.

CHAPTER SEVENTEEN

When I wake up, my cheek is vibrating. It's so weird. Why is it doing that? *And why am I so warm?*

It takes me a moment to figure out what's going on but slowly I start putting together the pieces. Two arms are wrapped snuggly around me, holding me close. Someone is snoring softly near my ear, it must be Beast.

I'm sitting sideways on his lap. I vaguely remember him grabbing me up and holding me while I cried myself to sleep.

I pull back my head and my cheek stops vibrating. I was using his chest as a pillow. That wet spot on his shirt must be from me. Oops. I guess I slept so well I drooled.

It's still dark but not as dark as I remembered. Beast's eyes must be closed because there's no red glow. Now that I'm awake, I can't fall back to sleep. I don't know quite what to do with myself except for to stay where I am. And if I have to be completely honest, I'm reluctant to leave the sanctuary of his arms.

Here, with him, I'm safe and protected. Nothing will hurt me. I have nothing to fear.

Carefully, I lean back until I can peek up at his face. His eyes are indeed closed and his face is relaxed even though his arms are tight around me. He must feel safe with me, otherwise I don't think he would have fallen asleep. He's left himself vulnerable and unprotected. *I could do anything to him.*

I reach out, and before I even understand what I'm doing, I'm touching him. My fingers brush first across his cheek and then they trace the line of his jaw. Even now, I'm awed by the silky feel of his purple skin. He's so hard and intimating, I still expect him to feel just as rough and hard as he looks.

I don't know why I'm doing it, it's crazy. I know I'm just asking for trouble by leading him on. I just have the strongest urge to touch him, I can't stop myself. It's as if my fingers woke up with a mind of their own.

His snoring ceases and for a moment, I think I've awakened him. His face remains relaxed. I watch him carefully for any signs of consciousness. When he doesn't open his eyes or try to stop me, my exploration continues on.

Down my fingers go, caressing the length of his neck. I pause at the hollow of his throat and lean in close. Breathing deep, I fill myself with his scent. He smells like the night air, musk, and the black roses that grow in my garden back home. *Home, don't think of home.*

There's only right now and right here.

My mouth is so close to his skin now, I have the craziest desire to find out if he tastes as good as he smells.

I part my lips. My breath blows over his skin. At the last moment, I catch myself.

What is wrong with you, Ameia? You can't just lick a sleeping alien without his permission.

I pull back and look up. His red eyes beam back at me. I feel like I just got caught stealing candy from the candy jar.

"Good morning," I stammer out.

I lean back and drop my hands to my lap. I don't know what I was doing or what came over me. *I don't understand why every time I touch him it tingles.*

Beast just stares at me all intense and very silent. It makes me feel so uncomfortable here, trapped, sitting on his lap. I can't help but squirm. The way he's staring at me makes me feel like he's scrutinizing me. Even if he isn't scrutinizing me, I feel so damn guilty for taking advantage of him.

"I'm sorry," I apologize and drop my eyes in shame. "I shouldn't have touched you while you were sleeping."

I'd be pretty pissed if I woke up to him touching me.

I expect him to be mad at me. I expect him to growl and grumble and voice his displeasure even though I don't understand him. I certainly don't expect him to kiss me.

Our lips collide as his head comes down and it feels like we're crashing into each other. Every thought that was running around in my head, every breath that was left in my chest is suddenly gone. Poof.

All that exists is him and the parts of me that are touching him. Lights flash behind my eyes, jolts of electricity travel down my thighs, and my body burns as if it's on fire.

His mouth moves over my mouth. Hot, wet, and hungry.

And all I want is more.

This moment, this pleasure, is all that I have, it's all that matters. It feels so good to be wrapped in his arms, to have his lips pulling at my lips. Life has sucked for so long now, I just want to feel good.

Hungry and demanding, his lips urge my lips to open for him. Suckle by suckle, he lulls me into relaxing against him. I part my lips and our tongues clash. I swear it feels like I was just struck by lightning.

It's unreal and almost too much. Too much sensation shooting down my spine. Too much pleasure warming my belly and spreading to my core. I can't breathe, it's like I'm drowning, drowning in feelings, tastes, and kisses.

I try to pull away from him, but his arms only tighten. There's no escape. I wanted this, I practically begged for it. I started the fire, now I have to feel it burn.

His tongue moves in my mouth, caressing and stroking, leading my tongue until I pick up his heady rhythm. Honey, he tastes like warm honey, I vaguely realize. *When was the last time I tasted something so sweet?* He's delectable. His taste is utterly intoxicating. I can't help but want more and more.

My hands reach out, clutching at his shirt. I feel like I need to hold on as he pushes himself deeper and deeper into me. He pushes until I feel the floor beneath my back.

Beast never stops kissing me as he bends me backward and then comes down on top. At first, he hovers above me. Then, as I arch my body off the floor, aching to be closer to him, he comes down. The weight, the pressure, it's like it scratches some deeply buried inch. I revel in the feel of him. Every inch of my skin that his skin touches sings with the pleasure of being beneath him.

His chest vibrates harder, thrumming against my breasts. I break the kiss, I can't help it. I cry out inside his mouth. He groans and swallows it.

His lips glide down my mouth to my throat. If I thought him kissing on the mouth was intense, when he kisses my neck, my body is sizzling. But then he goes further. What's left of my shirt goes up. His hot mouth covers my breast.

"Beast!" I cry out in surprise.

Hot, wet sensation. I'm melting, my nipple is a goner. His teeth scrape against it then he traps it and works it between his teeth.

He's trying to kill me. I'm going to *die*. Currents of white hot electricity are pulsing through me, all of it gathering in an unbearable throb between my thighs.

"Please," I groan out and wither beneath him. I'm asking him for something but I don't know what I want.

His teeth release me and even though it's a relief, the throb continues to pulse.

Down, he kisses. My tummy tightens. I find myself holding my breath. He undoes my pants and then they're gone.

Everything is happening so fast, it feels like I'm skipping seconds. His fingers dig into my hips. I feel him lifting me up, but I don't know why. *Why is he down there? He should be up here kissing me.*

Then he kisses me *there*.

"Oh, my stars!" I scream out.

I want him to keep doing what he's doing, but my hands start slapping at the top of his head as if they want him to stop. He ignores me and keeps kissing me. He only stops to slide his tongue through my folds. Not only does his tongue lick and lap at me, it vibrates as well. I think I'm going to completely unravel, he's ripping all my seams out. Then his mouth covers and pulls back a hard suckle from my swollen clit.

"You're a beast," I cry out.

The sensation is just too much for me to contain. It's so intense it hurts. My heart is going to explode, it's trying so hard to keep up with all the blood pumping to my clit. There's so much pressure now building inside me, I don't understand what's going on. I don't know how this is going to end.

Building and building, I'm so achy, I'm so needy, but I don't know for what. I can't stop moving, my thighs tense and relax around his head. Then my hands stop slapping, I grab him by the hair to trap him. To keep him right there, in that perfect spot.

Up, up, I'm climbing, I'm no longer of this world. The thread inside me is stretching, tightening, humming taunt. For a moment, at the top, I feel like I just might be okay. Then the thread snaps.

What goes up must come down, and oh, is the fall glorious.

I scream, I cry. My fingers tear at his hair as I buck off the floor. My sex convulses. My body spasms. He holds me through all of it.

His fingers dig into my hips while his tongue laps up my wetness. I'm melting, I'm gushing. He makes little noises in his throat. I feel like I've pleased him as he swallows me down.

When the last tremor passes and I feel like I can breathe again, his head pops up. His red eyes are glowing brighter than ever before.

"Mine," he growls.

My heart skips a beat.

My legs are trembling with the aftershocks.

He climbs up my body and hovers above me.

I realize my fingers are still tangled in his hair.

"I'm sorry, I didn't mean to hurt you," I apologize as I pull my fingers from his hair.

His dark lips curl into a pleased smirk. I feel my cheeks flushing with embarrassment.

Something passes between us. We're sharing a moment.

Beast strokes my cheek and growls.

I stare up at him. He stares down into my eyes as if expecting something.

He growls again and I almost think he's asking me a question. I wish I could understand.

Suddenly, Beast's face falls and I have the worse feeling that somehow I disappointed him.

Did I do something wrong?

He rolls off me, then like a true gentleman, he offers me a hand up.

***

What was that? How did I let that happen? How did I let him do those things to me?

My cheeks feel like they're on fire. I know I'm blushing from top to bottom. Part of me is embarrassed by what happened. I feel like I've exposed myself. I feel like I let a piece of myself go, and I'll never get that piece back. I lost all control of myself and he witnessed it. He did it.

Does this change everything between us now? Because I let him do that, will he think I've accepted his ownership of me? I don't know. And I don't know how I feel about what's between us. In the heat of the moment, I relished in the release. I wanted to be his. I wanted him to be mine.

It frightens me more than if it were to suddenly start raining feral fuzzballs and nightmare piggies.

His hand tightens around my hand and Beast looks at me with such longing it steals my breath. I find myself thinking it would be so easy to lift up on my tiptoes and capture his lips in a kiss. It would be so easy to throw myself against him. To revel in the warmth and strength of him. It would be so natural to see what other heights I can reach in his arms.

His eyes flash as if he can see exactly what I'm thinking. Abruptly he drops my hand and turns away.

I feel confused like I've done something to displease him. Just the thought makes me sick to my stomach. *What did I do wrong?*

He has a power over me, and he can wield it again and again. In his arms, I could lose myself.

I'm all that I have left.

I stare hard at his back. Even here, he doesn't look as if he belongs to this strange world. He's all purple and dark, clad all in black. He clashes too much against the blue-green of the foliage. The suns bright yellow rays don't bounce off his massive form, it's as if he absorbs them, shrouding himself in his own personal darkness. He looks as if he belongs somewhere in the shadows. Or some kind of Hell.

I shiver and walk over to the backpack I left on the floor. I pick it up and suck tiny sips from its spout. I'm thirsty, it's hard to not drink more. I know, though, that unless I pace myself, I'll really have to relieve myself.

Since I've crashed, I've had to make decisions I never had to make back home. Survival is growing more and more tiresome.

So what if I let go? What if I were to give myself to him? Would it truly be that bad?

I already feel drawn to him, like he has his own gravitational pull I'm too weak to resist. The way he touches me, the way I long to feel my skin against his skin, it's a slow kind of torture to keep denying myself. Life is already miserable enough as it is. Why should I make myself miserable?

Maybe I should just fall and get it over with. It would be so easy to let go.

But I can't even understand him. If a rescue comes for me, I could and would take him back home. I couldn't bear to leave him here, all alone. But unless he can learn to speak a language I can understand, I'm doomed to only guess at his intentions. Who is he? Where is he from? How did he get here? He could be a genocidal warlord for all I know. He sure looks the part.

Beast walks stiffly to the edge of the floor. Just watching him do it makes me as anxious as if I was doing it myself. I don't know how he can stand on the edge like that without fear, without becoming overwhelmingly dizzy and lightheaded. He stands there, staring off in the distance for a long time. I half expect him to sprout a pair of leathery black wings from his back and fly off into the horizon.

Just when I think I should do something to get his attention before my wild imagination gets totally out of hand, he turns back to me. His brows are pulled down and his lips are forming a scowl. I offer him the backpack. He shakes his head then points to the ladder.

It's time to descend.

My knees feel like they're made of rubber and it's a long climb down. The sun is high in the sky, daylight is burning. I don't know what Beast has planned for the day, but I hope it's to stop by my pod before we return to his ship.

We both straighten our clothes and get ourselves together. Physically, I feel relaxed, like something tight inside me has uncoiled. If anything, Beast seems even more wound up. I feel a little bad that it doesn't seem like he got any relief from all of our kissing. If anything, the aura around him seems even more intense now.

Beast starts down first and I climb after him. Going down is so much worse than going up. I don't know how many times I feel like the rung isn't where it's supposed to be. Every time my foot fails to connect, it feels like my stomach dropped out. More than once I feel like I'm about to splat against the ground.

When we finally reach the bottom, I find myself looking up of all things. I almost can't believe I ever made it up all the way up there, that I stayed all night there. *That Beast did those amazing things to me up there, in a tree.*

Then I look back down and see all the carnage that remains. The things that Beast killed still litter the ground. I don't know what they are, some strange scaly creatures who look like they were cooked up in a freaky nightmare. Beast is impatient, so I don't get to better examine them. He grabs me by the hand and we pick our way around the bodies, being careful not to step on them. When it's all clear, when the guts and blood no longer soak the ground, he rushes me through the forest.

CHAPTER EIGHTEEN

I'm so turned around after everything that happened, I have no clue where we're going.

Mercifully, Beast gives me a moment to find a tree and take care of my business. Then we're off again, rushing through the forest as if time itself is running out.

Once my bladder is empty, it's like I have more room for thoughts. I start to imagine what it would be like to take Beast home with me. I can just picture the look on Vrillum's face. I can just imagine the look on my father's. It would almost make this entire ordeal worth it.

Almost.

I feel like shouting *hallelujah* when we reach the break in the trees and I can see my pod right where I left it.

I'm anxious to see if I have any messages. My paces picks up, I almost rush past him.

I don't know why, after last night, that I have hope again that I'll somehow be able to make contact with back home. I guess to me my escape pod represents hope.

Ever since I've hooked up with Beast, my situation just keeps getting better and better. He's like the best thing that happened to me since I crashed. You know, besides all the wanting to own me stuff. He's like my hunky purple lucky charm. If I hadn't been so afraid of him in the beginning, this whole ordeal wouldn't have sucked so bad. When I think about it, he's done so much for me. He's fed me, sheltered me, and protected me. I want to return the favor by getting us a rescue off of here. After all, two heads are better than one.

My pod is much the same as I left it. I try to rush in, but Beast holds me back. He insists on entering first.

The pod is so small, there's nowhere to hide. If there was anything lurking inside, we would easily spot it. After Beast steps in, and does a quick inspection, there's not much room left for me. The space feels so much smaller with him filling it. It didn't feel nearly as small when it was just me. There's also a smell I don't remember, a distinct dirty princess funk I must have been accustomed to. I don't know how I stayed cooped up inside of here for so long.

Beast bends over my dashboard, checking it out. I let him examine it while I squeeze past and check on what I left behind in my storage box.

Right away I can see that something got in the box. Whatever it was got to the meat stick I left and gnawed it up into tiny splintered pieces. None of the rations bars seem to have been touched, however. Even the local wildlife knows it's not really food.

Beast pushes a button and the walls go up.

"Do you know how to work it?" I ask, turning to face him.

With the walls up, it feels even more cramped in here. His head nearly touches the ceiling, his shoulders span across the space between the seat and the dashboard. I'm trapped between the wall and the lock box.

Beast shrugs and pushes another button. The siren starts to blare. Ugh. Thankfully he quickly pushes that button again, turning it off. Unfortunately, my ears are ringing now.

Beast continues to experiment with the buttons. He learns how to turn the surveillance system on, even learns how to project his grunts and growls. He figures out how to raise and lower the small section of wall so that it functions like a door and he even manages to flash on and off the inside lights.

The only thing he manages to do that I never did is adjust the climate control.

"Beast?" I ask as he experiments with the climate control.

It gets sweltering hot and sweat breaks out on my brow.

I still get the feeling he's upset with me. I still feel like somehow I've made him mad, and the way he's ignoring me just reinforces it.

He holds the button down and the temperature becomes more manageable.

"Beast?" I have to repeat. "Will you turn around and look at me for a moment?"

He turns his face to look at me though it seems like he's slow and reluctant to do so.

"Do you think you could figure out how to send out a distress signal?"

His eyes harden and I feel like the weight of them are pushing me down. I almost back off. I almost say *nevermind*. I can see it. I can see it in his eyes that he's telling me not to go there. I should back off now, but we've come so far. I know I can make him understand.

My mouth goes dry and I have to clear my throat. Then I lift my chin in the air and pull my shoulders back.

"If we can get a message to my father, asking for a rescue...."

I don't get to finish. As if he's possessed, as if he's the very space demon I feared him to be, he growls and pounds the console with his fist. The panel of buttons cracks.

I recognized the warning just a moment ago, I knew he was telling me to back off. I just couldn't have expected this reaction. He's beyond mad.

I gasp in complete shock. Is this really happening? *He didn't just do that… he wouldn't…* But Beast isn't done. He pounds the panel of buttons again, shattering it where his fist connects.

"What are you doing?!" I cry out.

He turns his back on me. I gasp again, this time in outrage. He starts to tear the buttons off. Bits of plastic go flying, bouncing off the walls, bouncing off Beast, and clattering to the floor.

"Stop!" I scream at him.

But he keeps on going.

He's destroying it. He's destroying my only hope of ever getting home. Even if there's no way to send a distress signal, I know there's a GPS hardwired in the system. If he destroys it unless someone is already en route to this location, I'll never be rescued. I'll never walk on my home planet again.

Beast ignores me. He grabs the side of the dashboard. I watch in horror as his alien strong hands crunch into it, his fingers just sinking into the edges. Then he yanks back, ripping the entire dashboard out.

The siren goes off, the lights flash, and half the walls fall down.

Beast starts beating the screen, starts beating all the parts that are jutting out and every little bit that is left of the dashboard.

I'm pelted with pieces of plastic, pieces of metal, and multicolored buttons. I have to crouch down and shield myself with my hands.

"Stop!" I cry out. When that doesn't work, I try pleading nicely, "Please stop! Please!"

It goes on and on. Each crash, each crunch is like a punch to my soul.

Beast continues to beat my pod, continues to growl, tear, pummel, and punch until the siren chokes out.

I cower and protect myself. He's so enraged, I have no idea if he'll turn on me and start pummeling me as well.

When it's all done, when I only hear him panting and huffing, I dare a peek up. His shoulders are bent forward, and he's leaning against the wall, spent.

Shakily, I get to my feet. Through the blur of my tears, I take stock of the destruction. It's all gone, all of it. He smashed it all to bits. My hopes and dreams are scattered everywhere. I'll never be able to repair them.

I was foolish to believe that he would help me. I was so naïve and stupid to put any of my hope in him. How could I have thought he would help me get home?

How could I have believed he's any more than the Beast I dubbed him?

"I hate you," just pops out of my mouth and the next thing I know, I'm saying it again and again.

"I hate you!" I scream and bend over, grabbing up pieces. "I hate you!" I start throwing the broken remains of my console at his head.

"I'll never forgive you for this!"

He pushes away from the wall and makes a grab for me. If I wasn't trapped in such a small space, I might have been able to escape him.

He grabs my wrist and squeezes, the jagged piece of plastic I was holding falls from my hand.

"Mine," he growls.

With my other hand, I reach up and slap him across his big purple face.

"Never!" I scream at him.

I'll never be his. I'll never forgive him. I'll never forget this.

Beast doesn't even flinch. His face darkens where I slapped him, so I know I hit him hard enough to leave a mark, but he appears to be completely unfazed by it.

He captures my other hand and holds me as if it was nothing to him. I'm just a puny human, what am I next to the strength of the mighty alien?

I do the only thing I can do. I drift closer to him. The space between his brows wrinkles with confusion.

I lift my knee and jam it as hard as I can into his big purple nuts.

Beast's eyes glaze over and his grip relaxes around my wrists, but not enough to let me get away. There's more than physical pain twisting his features. For a split second, I could swear he looks like some hurt, demon puppy dog, staring at me with its wide, vulnerable eyes, not understanding why I just kicked it.

So I knee him again.

This time he lets go. Clutching his groin, he doubles over in pain, coughing and gagging. I know I have only seconds, if that, before he recovers. I grab on to the half raised wall beside me then throw myself over it.

I land hard on my knees against the solid ground. The sting that bites my knees gives me pause. I waste precious seconds blinking back tears while I struggle to my feet. Once I have my feet beneath me, though, I run as if the Devil himself is on my heels.

Don't look back.

CHAPTER NINETEEN

There's nowhere to run but to the trees. Thanks to Beast, my pod was rolled and positioned until it was completely surrounded by them. There isn't even a path that I can follow.

I swerve through the forest, my body fueled only by sheer desperation. I've only covered a couple of spans when Beast's roar blasts behind me.

I'm not going to make it.

My lungs are already laboring, burning with every breath. My legs feel impossibly heavy as if they're made of lead. My knees are screaming as they pump with every step. Still, I give it my all. I have nothing left.

I push through the pain. Mentally, I urge my body on. Spots flash in front of my eyes. My nose stings as if I snorted water. I can't give up even knowing I don't have a chance. I just can't.

Ominously, the sky grows darker as the trees thicken, growing closer and closer together. Beast rumbles behind me. I can feel his vibrations through the ground.

Just knowing that he's right behind me gives me a boost but it's not enough. I cry out as he grabs me and my feet leave the ground.

If only I was bigger, stronger, smarter…

I screech, slap, and kick my legs. I refuse to make it easy for him.

His breath puffs hotly in my ear. The bulges in his arms flex. He's squeezing the air out of me.

If only I wasn't me.

The spots flashing in front of my eyes grow brighter until they begin to burst.

I feel myself slipping away, his darkness is pulling at me.

Beast whispers softly into my ear. In my current, delusional state, it almost sounds as if he's apologizing to me.

His darkness swallows me up.

Is he sorry?

***

I wake up, I'm bouncing. My head aches. I can't see straight. Everything is blurry and upside down.

Something hard keeps jamming me in the stomach. It takes me too long to realize its Beast's shoulder. He's carrying me again.

Maybe it's the rhythm of the bouncing, or maybe it's because I feel exhausted and broken, but at some point, I end up falling asleep again.

The next time I wake up, I'm alone, tucked in the covers of his soft bed. *Was it all just a bad dream?* It wouldn't be my first.

Ripping the covers back, I swing my legs over the edge of the bed.

It wasn't a dream. My shirt is torn, exposing my ribs, and I'm wearing the black pants. I check my belt, it's still there, but the knife is missing from the sheath at my hip. *Dammit.*

I bend over and bury my face in my hands. My head is throbbing, my eyes are swelling with unshed tears. This sucks so bad. I don't know what I'm going to do.

How could he do this to me? I still, after everything, am having a hard time wrapping my brain around Beast's betrayal. I thought we were really getting somewhere, that we were making progress. I felt like I was finally beginning to understand him, and I was even feeling more open, more accepting of the thought that perhaps being with him, being his, wouldn't be so bad...

Why? Why? Just keeps looping in my head. I can't make any sense of it. *What did I do?*

He's fed me, sheltered me, washed me, and even bled for me... Silly me, I was beginning to think he really cared. I was even feeling guilty for not returning the favors.

Maybe that's it. Maybe it's because I did nothing for him but take everything he had to give. Was him destroying my pod his way of punishing me? Did he just get so fed up with me, he had to take from me the only thing I had?

Now I'm trapped here, with him, forever. The realization sends a cold shiver down my spine. I need him. I need his food, shelter, and supplies. I can't leave him, no matter how much I want to. I know what's out there and I have no way to protect myself from it. I'm not foolish to think I can somehow survive on my own.

What am I going to do?

CHAPTER TWENTY

I'm terribly depressed. Since, I've crashed on this planet, I've kept myself going on hope. There was always the possibility, always the chance that someone could find me and rescue me. I just had to survive long enough for it to happen.

Now, what do I have to live for? What is there to keep me going?

The prospect of ending my days here just increases my depression. I can't, I just can't even face the fact that Beast will probably still treat me as if I'm his. The thought makes me mentally and physically ill. If he touches me, ever again, I will totally freak.

I hate Beast. I hate him for what he did. If he was merciful, he would put me out of my misery. *If he was merciful, he wouldn't have done this to me.*

I curl back in bed and sleep. That's all I want to do. I want to sleep and forget this living nightmare I'm trapped in. For a while, I think I would be more content to live in my dreams. In my dreams, I can be anything. I can be anywhere. I can be happy. But my dreams take a turn for the worse.

I dream of Beast crushing his fist against my console. I scream at him to stop. I scream at him to stop hitting me. When he's done punching, Beast just walks away. I approach my console, to assess what he left me. The battered remains drip blood and look a lot like broken pieces of my face.

I wake up with a scream.

***

It takes some time for the terror to fade away, but when it does, I notice for the first time that the door to my room is left wide open.

That couldn't have been an accident…

I slip out of bed and tentatively drift towards the door, half expecting it to be some kind of trick. When I reach the opening, I peek out. The hallway beyond is empty, cold, and eerily silent.

Is this some kind of test? If I walk out there, is he going to take it as a justification to jump me?

I hold my breath and my ears strain, as I listen for any sign of him.

It feels like I'm in my pod again.

Waiting, always waiting. Afraid to make the wrong move. Afraid of making a hasty decision. *Afraid he's going to get me.*

I take one step out, then another. Nothing happens so I take some more steps until I'm sneaking cautiously down the hall.

All the doors that I pass are closed. I pass door after unmarked door until I reach the bathing facilities. The door to the bathing facilities is open. I stop and peek my head in. I half expect Beast to be in there, waiting for me. Or, even worse, he could be taking a bath. My eyes sweep through the room, ready to dart away should I see anything moving, but thankfully it's empty. I move on down the hall.

I keep going. Around the corner, this feels awfully familiar. I smell it before I actually see it. I reach the mess hall and its door is also open. I peek my head in.

The mess hall is empty, but a plate of food has been left on a table. I wouldn't normally presume that the food left there is for me or presume I have a right to take it but Beast and I had a habit of using the same table every time we ate. The plate of food is in front of the spot I always sat in.

My stomach grumbles, bubbling with hunger. It's probably been a day since I've eaten. Even knowing Beast obviously left that plate of food there for me to eat, stubbornly, I don't want to eat it. It feels too soon. It feels too like forgiving him a little if I eat it.

I turn to walk away. My foot is literally in the air when my stomach grumbles louder with distress. He left me a plate piled high with my favorite food: mystery meat skewers. It's taking more strength than I have to drag myself away.

Dammit. I can't starve myself forever. I have no way to gather or hunt my own food. *Unless he left the storage room open too.*

Now that thought gets me excited. It gets me so excited, I throw caution to the wind and rush out the door. My hunger is forgotten, my feet are practically flying as I run down the empty hall. I pass the front doors of the ship, they're closed. It doesn't matter. If I can get my hands on some weapons, I'll just bide my time until an opportunity presents itself. There are ration bars, water... everything I would need to hole up by myself. If I can get inside the storage room, I won't need him anymore.

I'm so wrapped up in my thoughts, in all the possibilities, and most especially the fantasy of freedom, that I'm not paying any attention to where I'm going. I turn a corner and crash hard into something solid.

I look up and recoil. It's him.

My teeth pull back and I snarl as I pick myself up off the floor. Beast reaches out to me as if he's going to touch me. I quickly scramble backward.

"Don't touch me!" I snap.

Beast takes a step toward me, he growls softly.

I turn my back on him and run back down the hall. I just can't deal with him right now. I can't stand to look at him.

My stomach hates me as I run past the mess hall. Especially because the aroma of meat hits my nose as soon as I draw close. It's just another thing to be angry at Beast for, another thing he's done to hurt me.

It's his fault I'll be hungry tonight.

CHAPTER TWENTY-ONE

Time has returned to a crawl. With nothing to entertain or distract myself with, once again I'm left with only my thoughts. It's enough to drive me mad.

I'm depressed, hungry, and pissed off. It's a miserable combination.

Out of them all, I have to say, keeping the hatred alive is the worse. It's a fire that I have to keep feeding, lest it fizzle out to mere anger. I've kept the fire raging inside me, and so far, I'm the only one that's getting burned.

I fight my hunger for what feels like hours until I finally give up. I convince myself that if I let myself starve with stubbornness, he actually wins. I travel back down the hall, not only half starving but also very afraid that the food will no longer be there. Thank the stars it's still there.

I shove a skewer in my mouth first, for the walk back down the hall, then grab up the plate. I'm taking it all back with me to eat in my room.

I was only gone a minute, two minutes max. When I get back to my room, I swear I can smell Beast, even over the delicious aroma of the charred meat in my mouth.

He was in my room, I just know it. He must have done something. I do a quick sweep of the room with my eyes. There's something different about the bed.

I can't even have a minute to enjoy what I'm eating. I gulp down the bite I'm chewing, no longer tasting it, and cautiously step in. The bed is made now, and I know I left it a mess.

Why would he make the bed? From the doorway, I couldn't see it because it's lying completely flat. Two steps in, I can't believe it. I swear my eyes must playing tricks. I bend forward, rest the plate of food I'm still holding down on the floor and make a leap for the bed.

It's my dress. My pink, party gown I left behind in the forest. When I left it, my dress was pretty much reduced to rags. Now, not only does it look like Beast washed all the funk out of it but he also made repairs to it as well. It's not quite as good as new, he made the repairs with black thread, but you can tell he put a lot of effort into the stitches.

A small, choked sound comes from me as I lovingly pick it up by the straps. I thought I'd never see it again.

I still have something left in this world.

I gently lay my dress on the bed and take a step back. I long to wear it, I long to feel like my old self again, but I need a bath first. I'm smelling quite awful. Not mention there's an entire plate of food waiting for me on the floor, growing cold. It would be a sin to waste it.

It's almost painful to walk away from my dress. I fear that if I look away for too long, when I look back it will be gone, as if it were a mirage.

I sit down on the floor and tear into my meal. From down here, I can't see the top of the bed, so I stand up. I walk over to the bed and sit beside my dress. I can't help but think of Beast as I finish my meal and stare at it.

How can I stay mad at him? Already, the flames of my hatred have died down to tiny wisps. I'm not even sure I have the energy to build them back up. I could almost forgive him for this… almost.

Why did he have to go and destroy my pod? A new wave of desperation washes over me. It's just as bad as the hatred.

I have to stop thinking of Beast. I have to stop trying to understand. It doesn't make sense. Unless he can explain to me, himself, I'll probably never understand. If I want to survive, I know the only things I should be thinking of are how to find a way to survive without him.

I can't rely on him. It felt great to rely on him, to put the burden of my needs on his broad shoulders, but he's a loose cannon. I need supplies, shelter, and a plan.

But first I need a bath.

I gently pick up my dress and drape it over my arm. The soft, silky skirt flutters as I walk out the door and down the hall.

The bathing facilities are empty though the air is steamy, I think the bathing pool is always kept warm. I go about my business, taking care of my more urgent needs then get myself ready for a shower.

I'm still wary that Beast will jump out of the shadows at any moment, so I decide I'm better off in a shower stall. At the very least it will buy me a few seconds. I would love to take a long, relaxing soak in the bubbles of the bathing pool. But if I do that, I leave myself completely vulnerable and at his mercy if he walks in. I'm just better off in the privacy of a shower. It's quicker and easier.

I choose the stall furthest in the back. It's the biggest of them all. It has a bench for me to sit on and a place to hang my towels and my dry clothes. The door has a lock, but I know if Beast really wants to get in, it won't stop him. Still, I lock the door. It's the thought that counts.

The shower itself is a panel of buttons that all look the same and a dozen holes in the walls. If I stand in front of the holes and push the right buttons, I should get sprayed by a jet of water from each hole.

I have no idea what I'm doing. *Eeny, meany, miny, moe.* I push a button. I get blasted by a dozen jets of icy cold water. I shriek and push that button again. The water stops but I'm so cold, my lungs feel like they're frozen, unable to take in air. I try the button next to that button, hoping it will be the hot water. I get blasted by scorching hot air. I go from soaking wet to instantly dry.

I'm afraid to try again but it's either this or the great wide open bath. This time I push a button and jump back. Half the holes spray out water. I reach out to test the water with my hand. The water is still icy cold. I have to lean into the icy cold water to push the button again. In my haste, I think I pushed the wrong one because instead of turning the water off, the other holes spray water. The new water is boiling hot. I'm scalded and cold.

"Would it be too much to ask for someone to actually label the buttons?" I cry out in frustration.

I mean, seriously, someone could get hurt doing this. Like I am.

I decide the shower isn't going to work. I'll just have to tough it out and take a bath. As much as I want to just abandon the shower and leave it as it is, I can't let the water keep running, even if the ship's water system will probably just recycle it.

I brace myself and focus on the two buttons I need to push. I jump forward and hit a button with each hand. The water turns off, it's only a couple of seconds of misery. But then the lights flicker then go out.

Shit, I broke the ship.

***

I'm in total pitch black darkness. I can't see my hand in front of my face. I blink my eyes and the scenery doesn't change. If the lights don't come back on, I'm screwed.

I wait a couple of minutes, nothing happens. All is quiet. I decide to slowly, and carefully, make my way to the door. The floor is slick with water. It makes not being able to see even worse. When the lights were on, I could swear I wasn't that far from the door. But now, in the darkness, with my arms and hands stretched out in front of me, there's only cold emptiness.

Where are the emergency lights? Any ship worth its salt has at least one system of emergency lights, if not more. Ah, but then I remember this ship is damaged.

My fingers make contact with something I don't expect. My gut clenches and my heart thunders. It takes me a second to realize it's not something to hurt me, it's just the skirt of my dress, which thankfully means I'm close to the stall door. I grab my dress and wiggle myself into it. Then I reach back out.

Two more steps and I find the door. My palms roam over the door, searching down, again miscalculating just where the lock is. I finally make contact with the lock, my fingers fumble with it, but I get the door open.

Inch by slow inch, my roaming palms guide me down the line of stalls as I try to make my way to the door. I feel like I'm halfway there, my pace even picks up because I'm more confidant when two red orbs suddenly appear. At first, they're small and far away. But as the orbs draw closer and closer, they grow.

"Beast?" I call out.

It has to be him, right? He's the only one with evil red eyes around here.

There's no answerback, only heavy silence that thickens the longer it goes on.

The red orbs grow larger and larger. I watch them as if I'm entranced. The orbs wink out.

I can sense something moving in the darkness. I'm in danger and every primal instinct in my body knows it. My heart races with icy panic. I start to walk backward until I feel like I just accidently hit a wall.

Beast growls and I scream.

A warm hand slams over my mouth.

Beast growls into my ear. Relief floods through me. I backed into him. It's his hand covering my mouth.

Beast grumbles softly and removes his hand.

"Why are the lights off?" I ask.

His hand slams back over my mouth.

Beast growls into my ear. I'm guessing he wants me to be quiet. I nod my head.

He drops his hand from my mouth and finds my fingers. I feel that familiar jolt of warm sensation shooting up my arm. The sensation is completely unwelcomed and couldn't be more unwanted. I have no choice but to suffer it, though. Beast is my only safe way out of here.

He starts to tug me and I follow him. It feels like it's the wrong way to me, but he is the one who can see in the dark. Slowly, cautiously, it feels like it takes forever to get where we're going.

After some time, I can see a crack of light in the distance. As we get closer, I can see the crack of light is coming from the front doors. No wonder it feels like it's taking forever to get out of the bathroom. He's already leading me down the hall and towards the exit.

Once we reach the front doors, Beast drops my hand and approaches a panel on the wall. I think he engages the emergency door functions because after pushing a sequence of buttons, he walks up to the doors and manually pulls them open without any mechanical assistance.

As soon as the doors open, I get blasted in the face with bright, harsh sunlight. I squint and cover my eyes. I need a minute to adjust.

Beast grabs my other hand and pulls me forward.

I stumble after him, "Hey, what's going on?"

Beast yanks me close and covers my mouth. *Why does he want me to be quiet?*

This time he doesn't growl in anger, he hisses. *What the heck is going on?*

I nod my head. I'll be good. I'll be quiet. I look at his face. I can't see his eyes. He's wearing a pair of dark glasses that hide them. Weird. His hand drops and he turns around, pulling me after him across the grassy exposed hills. He has not one, but two guns strapped to his back.

I have to wonder if he's expecting trouble.

We reach the line of trees and Beast chooses the biggest one to hide us behind. We get positioned behind the tree just in time. A mere moment later, I hear a loud pop as if someone popped a giant bubble.

I peek around the tree and look up. There's a ship in the sky. Oh, my god, there's a ship up there! Right now it's just a speck of black in a sea of blue. From here, I can't tell what kind of ship it is. *Am I being rescued?*

Beast suddenly yanks me back. His face gets up in my face. I can tell he's angry with me, the veins are bulging in his neck, but I don't know why. *Is he angry because I'm going to be rescued?* I eye his guns. *Does he think he can stop it from happening?*

I don't get to see the ship land, but I can hear it. The soft purring of the engines running is like music to my ears. *Freedom. Home.* I feel the vibrations in the ground as it lands. Beast turns his attention from me and raises his gun.

Now is my chance.

I know I can't outrun Beast. I'm not a complete idiot. I'm just hoping to get out far enough so those on the ship can see me and know that I'm here.

Beast is so focused on his gun, on aiming the ship down, I have the element of surprise on my side. I creep around my side of the tree then take off in a run.

"Ameia!" Beast yells out behind me.

It's so weird how he can say my name.

The ship, I can see now, has indeed landed. Though, I don't recognize the make or model. It's a mid-size, with a bullet-shaped body, and it's made out of black steel. The landing ramp drops to the ground. Beast still hasn't caught up to me, in fact, I don't think he's even behind me.

I make it half way to the ship before anyone appears.

"Ameia!" Beast yells again.

The first thing to walk down the landing ramp is an obsidian armored Ravager.

I stumble in surprised horror and tumble to the ground.

I can hear Beast yelling behind me as I fall to my knees. My hands, thankfully, manage to keep me from eating dirt. A burst of adrenaline floods my veins. *I'm going to die! The Ravager is going to kill me!* I push off the ground and scramble to my feet.

Beast appears from the line of trees and raises his weapon.

"Run! Beast! Run!" I scream and start running back to him.

Beast ignores me, he roars something in his alien tongue.

"If you're not going to run, then shoot them! Shoot them all!"

Beast fires his weapon. I see his body jerk from the recoil then everything goes black.

CHAPTER TWENTY-TWO

"You are not worthy of her. You should feel ashamed for sharing her air," a deep voice booms around me.

There is something strangely familiar about it.

I hear a growl but the growl is unfamiliar so it frightens me. I whimper and try to find my way out of the dark.

"See. You cause her distress," the booming voice says. "Begone from here."

"She is my Calling. I cannot help but want to be near her."

A warm hand touches my head, petting my hair.

"Do not touch her! She did not give you permission!" The booming voice thunders.

The petting of my hair stops. I whimper again, I actually kind of liked it.

"Did she give *you* permission to touch her?" the foreign voice asks.

There is only silence. The silence stretches on for so long, I fear I've fallen back into the blackness. I struggle to find my way back to full consciousness.

With a shrill gasp, my eyes open and I sit up.

I'm awake inside a nightmare. That's the only reason I can come up with to explain why I'm surrounded by dark, looming Ravagers. They tower above me, making me feel impossibly small. Impossibly weak and vulnerable.

A purple body breaks through the wall of black armor. I'm so relieved to see Beast, I start crying before I can stop it.

"Beast…" I sob and reach for him.

I just want him to hold me. To protect me from these monsters that have crawled out from under my bed.

"Ameia," Beast says and elbows the Ravagers out of his way.

There's grumbling and the elbowed Ravagers shuffle back, giving Beast room.

"Don't come any closer," the foreign voice behind me orders.

I peek a glance back and wish I hadn't.

There's a Ravager standing directly behind me. The Ravager covered head to toe in dull black armor, save for his hand. The sheen of his armor is dull. Instead of reflecting the lights, it seems like the armor absorbs it, shrouding the Ravager in his own personal cloud of darkness.

From the dark, two red eyes burn from his helmet. The helmet he wears has a wicked pair of horns sprouting from the top. The horns twist and the sharp tips are barbed. I've heard stories of them charging at their victims with their horns if they're disarmed of their guns. *How do they even shoot their guns when the fingers of their gauntlets are clawed?* That hand that is uncovered, that hand must have been the hand that was touching me. *Why is it purple?*

Beast stops coming for me, seemingly obeying the Ravager's order. He stands stiffly, only a foot from my bed. His fists clench at his sides and his red eyes are narrowed, glaring above me. I've never seen him look so pissed.

If Beast won't come to me, I'll go to him. Before I can think better of it, I jump out of the bed I'm in. I get both feet on the cold floor when I realize I'm tangled in a sheet. Still, I stubbornly try to take a step forward but the sheet clings to my legs and trips me up.

Two pairs of warm hands catch me, keeping me from falling to the floor. My body jerks, my insides spasm.

I cry out in half pleasure and half pain. Hot, electrical currents run amok inside my body. Zapping and jolting me, the currents of warm energy force their way through my veins, lighting me up.

It feels as if the hands holding me are bonding to me, fusing with my skin. No matter how much I twist and jerk, I can't escape them.

"Stop!" I scream.

One pair of hands drops. It's Beast's.

Beast sticks his hands in the air while backing away, to show me he's no longer touching me. Unfortunately, the other pair of hands is still glued to my skin. I can breathe, I can focus, but still, the pair of hands is sending thrilling jolts through me. More than enough to make me extremely uncomfortable. And very warm.

"Please stop." I twist around and look up at the cold helmet of the Ravager who is touching me. His purple hands are wrapped around my hips, squeezing me.

I look down at myself. All I'm wearing is the sheet snagged around my legs.

"Why am I naked?!" I try to cover myself with my hands. I cross one arm across my breasts and reach down, yanking the sheet back up.

"Let her go, Striker," Beast snarls.

My jaw drops. I can understand Beast.

"I can't," Striker groans behind me. His fingers tighten, his nails piercing my skin.

I whimper and try to tear myself away from him. He's hurting me.

Beast roars, enraged.

Beast drops his chin and suddenly charges Striker. As Beast's head connects with Striker's armored chest, I hear a loud crack. Striker's nails rip from my skin and the two fall to the ground.

I clutch my sheet to my chest and scramble away, but I have no escape. My hips are throbbing, I can feel blood trickling down my thighs. The circle of Ravagers around me pull in tighter, I'm complete surrounded.

Striker is protected by a full set of dull black armor, where Beast is not armored at all. This fight should be a no contest. If anything, I would think Beast would only be hurting himself. Yet, Beast is on top of Striker, growling and punching as if he's gone berserk.

Striker pushes at Beast, but he's unable to push him off.

Beast grabs hold of Striker's helmet by the barbed tipped horns. He rips the helmet off with a grunt, revealing a purple face that looks much like his own, red glowing eyes and all.

What the heck is going on? Is Beast a Ravager? Are all the Ravagers purple demons beneath their armor?

Beast tosses the helmet at the circle of guards. The helmet thunks off a breastplate and falls forgotten to the floor.

"She," Beast punches Striker in the face. "Did not," Beast punches him in the face again. "Give you," Beast punches Striker in the side of the head. "Permission!"

"Stop!" I scream.

The violence is making me sick. Beast made his point. Striker shouldn't have done what he did.

Beast's fist pauses in mid-air, he was about to punch Striker again. His head turns to me, his chest heaves with the force of his breathing. The way he huffs, the way he glares, I feel like gulping and taking a step back.

Beast pushes himself off of Striker and stalks towards me. His hands are clenched, the veins in his neck are throbbing, and he starts to drop his chin. For a moment, I fear he's going to charge me, just as he did Striker.

Beast stops just inches away from me and drops down to one knee.

Bowing his head before me, Beast says, "I'm sorry, princess. Please forgive me."

I so did not expect that. I blink then stare down at the top of Beast's head, unsure of what to say. I get the feeling he's asking me to forgive him for more than just this, for more than beating Striker to a pulp on my behalf. He's said he's sorry, he's asking for my forgiveness. Can I give it to him? Can I just let go of it all, just like that?

I clear my throat and look around nervously at the Ravagers encircling us. Everyone is watching. Even Striker is watching as he picks his bloody self off the floor.

I look back to Beast. He holds himself stiffly and the way he looks up at me... *How can red demon eyes look so vulnerable? So sad?*

As much as I want to continue to hate him for destroying my pod and for selfishly trying to keep me with him, after everything he's done for me, I just can't keep holding it against him. I've made my own mistakes. I'm not perfect. If he's willing to take on Striker, if he's willing to take on all these Ravagers, for me, how could I not forgive him?

Beast has proven himself time and time again. He will protect me. He will fight for me. I have a feeling, if he had to, Beast would take on this entire ship. I can see it the way he looks at me. I can feel it whenever I'm near him. If I just let myself trust him, I can count on him.

I'd be a fool to turn my back on him.

"I forgive you."

CHAPTER TWENTY-THREE

Just like that, I forgive Beast, and it feels as if some great weight has been lifted from my shoulders. I'm glad to be free of it.

Beast rises from the floor. If anything, he seems to grow and swell, more intimidating than ever before. He turns from me, and for a moment, I fear he may attack Striker again.

"You are relieved of duty, Commander Striker. I'm taking command of this ship," Beast says.

What? Did Beast just take over the ship?

Striker glares at Beast and snarls, "Yes, Sir."

"You are to report to me on the bridge in two hours," Beast continues.

Striker nods at Beast and with his thumb wipes blood from the corner of his busted lip. "Yes, Sir." His red eyes slide my way and he stares at me. The way he stares at me, his eyes burning with hunger even with his face messed up, I feel like I'm meeting Beast for the first time again. *Space demon.*

I shiver and clutch the sheet tighter.

Striker frowns at me before looking back at Beast.

"You are dismissed," Beast orders.

"Sir, what about…" Striker starts but Beast cuts him off.

"I said you were dismissed!"

I hold my breath, afraid that the two of them are going to come to blows again. Well, Striker didn't exactly hit Beast last time, Beast did all the pummeling. Beast looks almost eager for Striker to make a move. He shifts on his feet restlessly and the corners of his lips twitch as if he's just waiting for an excuse.

Striker looks back to me. I can tell he wants to say something to me. His lips start to part, but he must think better of it. He gives Beast a curt nod of his head and turns away from us. He walks the other way, bending down to pick his helmet off the floor. One of the horns on the helmet is now bent sideways and the side has a big dent in it. He shoots one last glare over his shoulder at Beast and slams the helmet over his head. Then he pushes his way through the wall of Ravagers, snapping, "Out of my way!"

"Ameia," Beast says softly, drawing my attention back to him.

I release the breath I was holding and feel my shoulders slumping.

Beast walks up to me and offers me his hand. I hesitate for only a moment before placing my hand in his. His fingers squeeze around me. There's comfort in his strength, there's familiarity in the jolt that shoots up my arm.

Beast's eyes roam hotly over me and I feel even more vulnerable and exposed in my flimsy sheet. If I could shy away from him, I would. He frowns, as if just realizing something, and let's go of my hand.

"Here," he says and yanks his own black shirt over his head. "Wear this."

He is literally giving me the shirt off of his back.

Gently, as if he was afraid of hurting me, Beast lowers the shirt over my head. With some creative wiggling, I manage to get my arms in without flashing any more of myself. The sheet falls forgotten to the floor. Beast's shirt is warm and soft. It hits my knees, fitting just like a baggy black dress. I feel much more respectable.

Beast's bare chest fills my vision. I can't help but admire all of his bulging muscles, especially his hard pecs. As I gaze upon him, his chest rises and falls just a bit quicker. He's breathing faster. I look up.

Our eyes lock, I just can't look away from him. How can he be so vicious to the world and so giving to me? He grabs my hand and I have to swallow back the sound of pleasure that jumps in my throat. I feel tingly all over.

***

Beast doesn't have to snap at the wall of Ravagers, they just move out of his way, parting like a black sea so we can pass. I have so many questions, I don't even know where to start, so I don't.

Beast leads me past the Ravagers, and beyond them, I can finally see we're in some type of medical area. There are rows of beds, much like the bed I woke up on. And purple men I assume are doctors, overseeing their prone purple patients.

So, these are Beast's people. So far, everyone not in armor looks a hell of a lot like him. Purple skin, red eyes, though some aren't glowing as brightly as others, and dark hair.

That makes Beast a Ravager. I sneak a sideway glance at him. I should be afraid but it actually makes a lot of sense. If anything, it's a bit of a comfort to know that he's just one of a whole species who are notorious for their murdering, plundering, and slaving ways. And not say an actual demon.

Yeah, I've been through a lot if I can find a bright side to murdering, plundering, and slaving.

Beast and I were pretty much ignored as we walked through the medical bay. The doctors and patients there must have been too busy to give us attention. As we walk down the halls, though, everyone we pass stops and stares.

"Sir…" Some of them say in disbelief.

Most don't say anything at all. They watch us with shocked faces and wide eyes. They run off, no doubt to share what they just witnessed. And soon the hallways are filled with unarmored and armored Ravagers alike, squeezing up against the walls, just to get a glimpse.

This, this I'm used to. Being gawked at. Crowds gathering just to get a look. But this isn't for me. I can see it. They ignore me even though I'm the one clearly out of place. Everyone, not only me, has eyes only for Beast.

Beast stares ahead, nodding only when someone says, "Sir." Otherwise, he's stiff and imposing. It's clear, he's not open for conversation at this point.

So many times I almost start to question him. There's just so many questions ready to jump from my tongue and fly past my lips. I almost chew my bottom lip raw from biting it.

After an eternity, Beast stops at a door and tells it to, "Open."

He ushers me in first then glares at all of the gawkers that linger, warning them to back off.

With Beast's warm hand against my back, I walk in first, barely looking at the accommodations. I can't wait another minute to find out what's going on.

As soon as the door closes behind Beast and we have privacy, I turn to him and say, "Okay, you have some explaining to do."

"Fire away, Ameia," Beast says as he walks past me and begins to inspect the room.

There are so many questions in my head vying to get out, I have to take a moment to pick one. I decide to start with, "Where are we?"

"We are presently located on my ship, the Harpy's Talon."

Beast walks over to a wall and starts pushing buttons. Drawer after drawer slides out, he looks in every single one of them.

"Your ship?" I ask.

He nods and says simply, "Yes, my ship," not giving me any clarification. He moves on to the other wall, pushing buttons and inspecting the shelves that pop out.

"How did we get here?"

"You don't remember?" he asks, not even looking at me.

"No. The last thing I remember is telling you to run then I woke up here."

"Striker shot you."

I gasp. *Of course he did that bastard.*

"If it makes you feel any better, I shot him."

"No, no that doesn't make me feel any better," I say but inside, it does make me feel a bit better. Just a little bit.

"How can I understand you now?" I ask and get tired of lingering by the door.

I walk further in and take in the room. First and foremost, it's obvious this room is meant for sleeping. There's a large bed in the very center, covered in pillows and thick blankets, taking up most of the space. All the other furniture only pops out of the wall when you push a button, then retracts when you push the button again. Otherwise, it would be impossible to walk around the bed, one would have to constantly crawl over it.

"I had my translator replaced. The old one was broken."

I walk up to the bed and take a seat on the edge. "So that's why you sounded like a dog…"

Beast turns to me and both his brows lift in interest, "I sounded like a dog to you?"

"Yes," I say, widening my eyes at him, "You just kept growling and barking at me. I couldn't understand you at all."

Beast laughs and soon I found myself joining him. The tension seems to flow out of me as I laugh, it's the first time we've shared a moment like this. It's the first time I've laughed in ages. However, it's only a moment and gone before I know it. When we're done, the silence that falls feels even heavier than before. The tension returns with a vengeance.

Beast stares at me, his eyes darkening, his breathing quickened.

I squirm on the bed and look away. I sense Beast move and then hear him continuing his inspection.

So many questions, but how do I work up the nerve to ask them?

Why do you look at me like that? *Why do I like it?*

If I ask him if he'll help me return home, will he go berserk and start destroying this ship?

"Why did you destroy my pod?"

Beast sighs, "I shouldn't have done that."

Perhaps it's his admission that gives me the courage to press. I peek up at him and find myself boldly saying, "That doesn't answer my question."

Inside, I brace myself for his reaction.

Beast moves away from the wall and walks over to the bed. He takes a seat beside me. The bed dips as his weight sinks into the mattress and I have to reposition myself, to keep from sinking with it.

"Ameia," he says softly, "Princess."

He reaches for my hand and I let him take it. My fingers tingle delightfully as his fingers slip between them.

"Your pod's system was infected with a suppressor virus."

"A suppressor virus?" I ask, confused. I feel just a little bit stupid for not knowing what it is.

"It's a virus that suppresses a ship's communication and navigation systems."

"Oh." I guess that would explain why no one came for me. "That was unfortunate." Perhaps I was wrong for blaming Vrillum for my situation.

"Yes," Beast agrees. "It was unfortunate."

"But it doesn't explain why you tore my pod to pieces."

Beast squeezes my hand then lifts it to his mouth. His soft lips brush across my knuckles. It feels like my skin comes alive beneath his faint kiss, pulsing with energy.

"Not being able to give you what you want enrages me."

"What? Why?" I ask. That doesn't make any sense.

"Because you are my Calling."

Instead of answers, I only have more questions. This whole thing is starting to become quite frustrating. I try to pull my hand back from Beast, him touching me is only distracting me. He holds tight to my hand, though, and bestows upon me another brushing of his lips.

"My name is not Calling."

"My name is not Beast."

My cheeks flame with embarrassment. That's right, Beast isn't his name. All this time, I've been thinking of him as Beast, addressing him as Beast, because that's what I chose to call him. Like he was a pet. I didn't even think to ask him his name. That should have been my first question...

"Who are you?"

Beast grins at me, his voice full of pride as he states, "I am Drek Ros Karmada, son of Ros Vin Karmada, King of Blackspire."

My mouth goes dry. The information is a lot to swallow. I lick my lips before asking, "So, you're a prince?"

His eyes seem to flare as they follow my tongue's slide across my lips. I instantly regret licking them. I also instantly regret letting him hold my hand.

"Yes, I am a prince, Ameia. And you are welcome to continue to call me Beast if you like, I've grown quite used to it. But if you prefer to use my proper name, you may call me Drek."

I feel so embarrassed it hurts. All this time, all this time he's been a prince and I never even guessed at it. Look at me, the princess in rags, yet I behaved many times as if I was above him.

"I'm sorry." I don't know what else to say. I can only hope he doesn't hold it against me. So far, it doesn't seem like he is.

"It's fine, Ameia," Beast says reassuringly. He treats me better than I deserve. "All is forgiven. Yes?"

"Yes," I confirm, nodding my head. "All is forgiven."

I so don't even want to know what other embarrassing stuff I did without even knowing it. For some reason, I start remembering what we did in the tree. How good it felt to have his head between my thighs. *His tongue is made of magic.*

"You are my Calling, Ameia," Beast says, his voice sounding somehow even deeper and husky, pulling me out of my thoughts.

I'm panting. Oh, my stars, I'm panting. *Get ahold of yourself, Ameia.*

"What is a Calling?" I ask. And how can I be his? Is he going to start calling me Mine again?

"You will lead me to my destiny," he says in all seriousness.

"How am I supposed to do that?"

Beast tips his head back and laughs. This time, I can't join him. Something about this doesn't seem like a laughing matter. It feels too serious.

"All you have to do is accept me."

"How do I accept you?"

"I'll show you," Beast says, his voice husky again. He bends forward and captures my lips with his.

Beast's mouth slants over my mouth and this time it feels as if he's taking his time. This time his pulls from my lips are slow and lingering. They grow deeper and deeper until I feel myself grabbing at him, pulling him closer, wanting more.

His tongue probes at my lips, seeking entrance. The first touch of his tongue is like a zap. I feel all my muscles tense, my body goes rigid, and my lips open for him with a gasp.

In, his tongue slips into my mouth. He's so sweet, so warm, my tongue eagerly slides against his. Beast groans now as I kiss him back, each stroke I return only spurns him on. Our tongues duel in an electric slip and glide as he attempts to kiss me into submission. Even his tongue is powerful, soon overpowering mine, only to then push me into keeping up with his dance.

My hands start to squeeze his shoulders, kneading in rhythm with the strokes of our kiss. I feel him stiffen as my fingers work him then his arms come around me, wrapping me up in an embrace. My hips are moving, I can't keep my body from squirming. I want something though I don't know what that something is. His strong hands roam down my back, pausing at my hips. Then they drop, and I feel him grabbing two big handfuls of my ass, squeezing, kneading in the same rhythm of my hands.

Just when I feel like my body has melted, my bones are liquid and my belly is full of heat, Beast tears his lips from my mouth, breaking our deep kiss. He reaches up, one hand tilting my head to the side. His fingers work their way into my hair and then grab it, trapping me. Then his moist lips lick and nip a hot trail down my neck. I can only moan softly my pleasure, feeling as if I'm caught on a live wire with no escape.

Sparks flash. My breathing is erratic. But he doesn't stop. His teeth graze across my collarbones then his other hand leaves my ass only to cover my breast. Even through the fabric of the shirt, I can feel the heat of his hand as he squeezes. I feel my nipple puckering under the press of his palm.

"Ameia," Beast breathes hotly against the wetness he left on my neck. "If you want me to stop, just say it."

I shiver, all the little hairs on my body feel like they're standing on end. Stop? Why would I want him to stop? It feels so good. I just want *more*.

"Don't stop, please," I breathe out, it feels like I'm breathing fire.

My hand covers his hand. I squeeze my fingers to make him squeeze my breast harder.

"Gods, Ameia," Beast groans.

My back arches, grinding my hard nipple into his palm. His breathing is ragged, he starts to kiss my neck with a new desperation. Suddenly his hand leaves my ass. I cry out at the loss of that pressure. His hands grab at my shirt, I hear stitches snapping. He rips the shirt open instead of pulling it over my head.

I know it's not cold in the room, but the air that hits my chest feels cool as it meets the fevered heat of my skin.

"You are so beautiful," Beast growls as his eyes drink me in.

I look down at myself, trying to see myself as he sees me. My skin is flushed pink, my nipples are tight rosy buds, and my breasts rise and fall steadily, heaving with my pants.

Beast makes a sound deep in his throat as bends down and buries his face between my breasts. First, I feel him breathing me in, filling himself with my scent. Then his face moves. His mouth sucks at the side of my breast before his tongue slides over the mound, ending with the tip of his tongue flicking across my nipple.

"Oh!" I cry out and shudder. It feels as if his tongue just zapped me.

He does it again. The tip of his tongue flicks, my nipple sparks, hot and alive with energy.

My back arches and I beg him for, "More."

Beast's tongue is so hot, so wet, as he drags it across me, making me squirm. It's such a sweet torture. I feel restless. I can't stay still. I grab at his hair. I yank, trying to pull him closer, trying to force him to give me more.

He fights me, he's dead set on taking his time, on torturing me. His tongue plays with me, swirling around, circling my nipple. His teeth just barely graze my tips. The tiny sparks, the pops of sensation are not enough. I need more of something... I just don't know what that something is.

"Beast, please," I groan. There's a throb growing between my thighs, pulsing and tormenting me. I'm so hot, all of me is melting. I fear I'll be reduced to just a puddle soaking his bed.

"Ameia, I've waited so long for this," his breath is hot against me.

I arch, if I bend my spine anymore, it's going to snap. He groans, it's a tortured sound, as if he's finding it just as difficult as I am.

His hands cover my breast. Squeezing, kneading. My head falls back, still I pull at him. Closer, I need him closer. I want to feel him against me, I want his skin against my skin.

Why does he resist?

"Please," I plead one last time. My eyes feel heavy. I look at him through my lashes.

Beast looks up at me. I think I'm getting through to him. He stares so long into my eyes, I feel like I'm getting lost in the red lights of his.

"Tell me what you want, my Princess," he huskily orders me. The way he says my Princess does funny things to my tummy. My heart flutters, to hear him say I am his.

"Do..." I have to think. How can I put into words the feelings I want him to give me? "What you did in the tree."

Beast chuckles huskily. His hands grip my breasts, tightening, constricting them delightfully. Then I feel him pushing me back. *Yes! This is just like what we did in the tree.* He looms above me, hovering. He so big, so wide, his shadow completely blankets me.

"Like this?" Beast asks.

"Yes," I breathe, my nails scratching down the back of his neck.

I feel him stiffen above me, then he arches as I scratch my way down his back, following the groove of his spine.

"Ameia," he growls. "Tell me what you want."

I pout as I reach his ass. He's still wearing his pants. I just have the strongest urge to tear my nails down his taut cheeks. Still, I scratch my way across the fabric. I feel him clench.

He growls again, "Tell me."

"I don't know," I sigh and squirm uncomfortably.

There's a feeling inside me, an ache that's not quite an ache. I don't know what will make it go away. I don't know what to do to make it happy.

Beast bends his head down and his teeth graze across my neck. "You want me?"

"Yes," I gasp. I don't think I'll ever get used to the shocks or the zaps of electricity. As his teeth nip me, scratching at me, it's as if there's a direct line of sensation flowing to the junction between my thighs. It's so intense, so raw, something inside me clenches.

"Tell me."

I dig my fingers in his cheeks. I want to pull him into me. I have the strongest urge to rub him against me.

"I want you," I say breathlessly.

"Do you want me to kiss you here?" he asks and then he sucks on the side of my neck.

The pulls of his mouth have me rising off the bed. "Yes," I encourage him. "Yes."

"And here?" he asks. His eyes peer up at me as his lips drag down to my breast. I hold my breath, waiting, aching.

"Yes, please, yes."

His molten mouth covers me.

"Stars!" I cry out, my eyes rolling back in my head.

He suckles hungrily on me. He's so hot, so wet. I can't stand it. I thought I wanted this, but it's only making the throbbing worse. I squeeze my thighs together. The pulsing between them vibrates down to my knees and up to my hips.

Beast pulls his head back and my breast leaves his mouth with a wet pop. He places hungry kisses down me. I hold my breath as his lips glide across my tight stomach. He reaches my belly button then his tongue stops to dip in.

"Why are you torturing me?" I groan out. I resist the urge to lift my hips. He's so close to me down there, I'll only be lifting them into him.

"This isn't torture, my sweet Ameia." Beast chuckles and his hands grab me by the hips.

"Then what is it?"

"This is me enjoying every inch of your sweet body."

The bed dips as he shifts his hard body over me.

"And kissing you until you accept me."

"Oh," I breathe.

His hands drag slowly from my hips down to thighs. His hands knead me, working at me, then slowly they push me open.

His voice catches in his throat as he gazes upon me, "Marvelous."

Beast doesn't hesitate. Like a man who's gone hungry, who's been starving, his mouth ravenously attacks me. First, he attacks the inside of my thighs. He sucks large mouthfuls of me in his mouth. He pulls back, bringing my blood rushing to my skin. Then he moves on, his tongue swirling up my thighs, stopping to trace the line, following the border until he crosses into my apex.

For some reason, I expect him to take his time like he did the first time, but he doesn't. Beast's mouth falls upon my sex, growling as he works his tongue against my folds. I'm so shocked, so surprised by the rush of heat that floods me, I'm paralyzed. Then his tongue laps across my clit.

"Beast!" I shriek. He chuckles and then his tongue starts vibrating.

It's too much. The throbbing is too strong. His vibrating tongue only makes it worse. My insides are boiling, all the pressure I feel must be steam.

I cry out, much like before, and grab at his head. I'm not sure if I'm trying to pull him off or trying to make him do more with his mouth.

His vibrating tongue traps my clit, smothering it. I buck against him, only making it worse. There's too much aching, too much need.

And just when I think it can't get any worse, I feel something probing and pushing to get inside me. One finger slips in. I feel myself clenching around it. His finger curls, stroking against a too sensitive spot.

I explode in a wet gush of release.

I scream and cry, my fingers tear at his head. At times, I call him Beast, at times I call him Drek. It's a wonder I can call him anything at all.

"Ameia," he purrs when it's all said and done.

Slowly, pieces of myself come back to me. My eyes were blind, but now they can see. I look down. His mouth is glistening. He runs his tongue along his lips.

That's me he's licking up.

"Wow," I sigh and I sink back, relaxing into the bed. My body feels weak and heavy. I couldn't move if I wanted to.

Beast crawls up me and I have the strongest sense of déjà vu. We've done this before but unlike last time, he doesn't just stare at me and leave. I feel his knee nudging at my knee. *What does he want?* I open for him.

He pushes himself between my knees. I feel the brush of something hard. I look at him, confused, not understanding what's going on.

"Aren't we done?"

Beast laughs, a tortured laugh, and then his face is suddenly serious as he growls, "Not yet."

What more can he want? Just the thought frightens me. I thought we were just going to do what we did in the tree, I didn't expect this.

"Don't be afraid, my Ameia," he growls but the way he looks at me, the way his red eyes flare at me, I can't help it.

He reaches down between us. I feel something hard brush against my folds and my hips jerk. I'm aghast to realize I'm even more sensitive.

I try to look down, but the space between our bodies is shrouded in darkness. "What's going on?"

"I need you to accept me," he says through clenched teeth.

I look up at him helplessly. "I don't understand what that means. Can you explain it?"

"Princess Ameia of Terrea," Beast groans. "You are my Calling." His hand moves between us, then I feel something hard rubbing against my folds.

I cry out. The throb awakens with a vengeance.

"Gods, you're wet."

"Beast... Drek," I cry, "What are you doing?"

"You and you alone will lead me to my destiny. I pledge to you my heart and my soul. I pledge to you my arms and my unwavering protection."

I feel so lightheaded, it's as if all the blood has rushed from my head, flooding the lower parts of my body.

"Everything that I have is yours. My kingdom. My people. My possessions. Me." He keeps rubbing, keeps sliding something hard between my folds, driving me crazy.

His other hand grabs me by the hair and he yanks so that my chin lifts and our eyes meet, "Do you accept my pledge?"

Do I accept him? This dark devil from space who has pledged to me everything that he has? Whose protected me, fed me, sheltered me, and fought for me? Not to mention he's literally given me the shirt off of his back.

The words, "Yes, I accept," barely make it past my lips before he thrusts something slick and velvety inside me.

I feel a pinch and then a tender soreness. I cry out in pain and Beast smothers it with his lips. His weight falls on top of me and I feel not only myself sinking into the mattress, but his purring chest vibrating against my breasts.

"Ameia," he pulls back. "I'm sorry."

I feel full of something long and thick but it doesn't move and the pain begins to ease.

Beast nuzzles against my neck. "I'm sorry. Please forgive me."

"I forgive you," I say softly.

The pain eases completely.

"You're so tight," he groans. "Does it still hurt?"

I feel the fullness withdraw from me only to suddenly fill me again.

"No," I breathe, arching my back.

"Good," he groans. "I… can't…hold back."

The man above me transforms before my eyes. Gone is the image of Drek holding himself back, replaced is a madman, the Beast I know so well. A frenzied animal. He grabs up my legs, encouraging me to wrap them around his waist. Then he attacks me. He pummels himself inside me. Driving every long inch of his inside me. The force of his body crashing into my body slams me into the bed.

"Mine," Beast growls. His teeth sink into my neck. It hurts so good. In my lust filled haze I can't get enough, I want to be marked by him.

He drives so deep my hips touches his hips. I start to scream when he starts slamming into my clit.

I swell and ache, throbbing with need. My hips buck, my body writhes beneath him. My head thrashes.

The purring in his chest grows stronger and stronger. My thighs tense and my stomach tightens. I feel my walls clenching around him, gripping him. Milking him. He cries out and I completely lose it.

It's not like before, it's so much better than when he licked me to release, but also so much worse. It's stronger, it's darker. It's painfully intense. For a moment, I feel like I'm dying. I can't breathe. My lungs won't work. My heart is racing. My blood is thumping. Energy crackles across my skin.

Then I realize I'm still holding on. If I just let go, this will all be over. Reality cracks. Something inside me breaks. I explode into a million, colorful, sparkling pieces.

"Mine," Beast says again, much more softly.

His hips are rolling against me. I feel him, him that is already almost too big, swelling inside me. Growing. He pulses, above me he twitches. He groans and I fill so warm. Hot wet heat is filling me up. I'm so full, I'm leaking.

Down, down I drift, my pieces falling back into place. Somehow they know just where to go, they know exactly where they fit.

I peer up at Beast as if seeing him for the first time. My body tingles with a warm kind of numbness.

He stares back at me, his own eyes wide and surprised.

I lift up and groan. It feels too raw and too tender as he twitches inside me. But still, I just gotta do this.

"Mine," I purr and press my lips to Beast's lips. I feel him smiling against my kiss. He wraps his arms around me and rolls over then positions me on top of him.

***

Beast's arm is heavy upon me. His body is curved around my body. I'm snuggled up comfortably against him. For the moment, I'm just savoring the feel and the newness of being intimate with him.

He sleeps peacefully, his breathing a deep, predictable rhythm. I'm a little jealous. I wish I could relax. My muscles are exhausted, my eyes are heavy, but I just can't sleep. Every time I close my eyes, I see home.

My father must think the worse. Does he think I'm dead? Does he wonder what happened to me? Is he still looking?

I can't help but feel guilty that I'm in a soft, warm bed with Beast while my family and my people don't know what happened to me. It would probably scare my father to death to know I'm on a Ravager ship. *How do I even tell him, if I even get the chance to tell him, that I joined with the Ravager Prince?*

The rhythm of Beast's breathing changes. He begins to purr. I feel his fingers stroking against my hip and his chest vibrating against my back.

"Drek?" I whisper. If he's not already awake, I don't want to disturb him.

"Yes, my princess?" his warm breath washes over my neck.

"May I ask you something?"

I feel him stiffen. "Of course."

I twist beneath his arm and roll over to face him. I can't ask this question with him at my back. I need to see his reaction.

I swallow. I've been wanting to ask him for what felt like hours while he was sleeping, but now that I actually have the chance, I don't know if I have the courage to go through with it.

I look down, focusing on a spot on his chest. "First, promise you won't get mad."

His fingers brush against my jaw, then he nudges my chin up to look at him. "I promise."

My eyes meet his eyes. I'm so grateful that we're actually able to communicate now. That I can ask him this and he can answer. I won't have to guess what his grunts or growl mean. I won't have to guess if he'll hate me for what I'm about to ask.

I take a deep breath. "This might make you mad..."

His eyes hold mine as he repeats, "I promise."

The last time I asked him about contacting home, he went berserk and destroyed my pod. I steel myself, seriously expecting him to break his promise and get pissed as I ask, "Will you take me home?"

"Of course," Beast says easily, too easily. "We're headed there right now."

***

ABOUT SARA PAGE

Want Sara Page books for free? Join her ARC Team:
http://dirtynothings.com/free-books/

Sign up with her mailing list to receive updates, announcements, and special offers.

Sara Page Mailing List Signup:
http://eepurl.com/2SdZ9

Sara Page's Website
http://dirtynothings.com/

Follow on Facebook:
https://www.facebook.com/authorSaraPage

Follow on Twitter:
https://twitter.com/AuthorSaraPage

Sara Page's Biography:
http://amazon.com/author/sarapage

Sara Page's Newotica Page:
http://newotica.com/c/authors/sara-page/

Other works by Sara Page:

Paranormal Romance Novellas

Luna's Captive
Luna's Howl
Luna's Bite
Luna's Heat
Moon Alley Alpha (Complete Moon Alley
series)

Erotic Short Stories

Sinful Bargain
A Sinful Bargain

Moon Alley Pack
Ravished by the Pack
Ravished by the Pack 2

Lana Murphy Series
Processed
Claimed
Stolen
Collared
Invited
Punished

My Arranged Marriage Series
The Wedding Night
The Honeymoon
Newlywed
Not So Merry Matrimony

Maybe Baby
Happily Ever After

Fulfilling His Secret Fantasy Series
A Dirty Game Among Friends
A Little Seduction Between Friends

Rekindle Series
Marriage Retreat

Rabid Lust
Diary of a Booth Girl

Short Story Bundles
Awake in a Dream (Lana Murphy)
Awake in a Dream 2 (Lana Murphy)
Submissive Pleasure (Submissive Stories)
More Than One Pleasure (Ménage Stories)
My Arranged Marriage Bundle

Made in the USA
Coppell, TX
18 July 2021

59142370R00131